A WOMAN'S PLACE

Also by Marita Golden

MIGRATIONS OF THE HEART

MARITA GOLDEN

A WOMAN'S PLACE

DOUBLEDAY & COMPANY, INC.
GARDEN CITY, NEW YORK
1986

Library of Congress Cataloging-in-Publication Data
Golden, Marita.
A woman's place.
I. Title.
PS3557.O3593W6   1986   813'.54   85-29397
ISBN 0-385-19454-4

This book is
for Tunde,
who I am teaching
to always walk
the way he does now,
as though he carries
his destiny with him
instead of hoping
to meet it along the way.

Once again, and always, thanks to Marie Brown, whose sharp eye and red pencil never miss a thing, and whose encouragement makes the solitude of my task worthwhile.

For the first time and always, thanks to Ifasola for helping me write a new chapter of my life.

A WOMAN'S PLACE

Faith

Winthrop University. Mama said she liked the sound of the name. Said it made her think of fine china, tweed suits and money in the bank. But I just looked at the pictures in the catalog they sent and wondered why I was supposed to want everything I saw. Because that's how mama made it sound. Like coming here wasn't my first chance, but my last one too. But nothing seems real. Not the teachers. Not the students. And sometimes, even me. If there was something here for me to believe in, I wouldn't be flunking out.

I remember the first time I went into Hawthorne Hall to take Western Civilization I. I caught my breath when I walked in through the door. And all these different smells and sensations hit me all at once. The ceiling was real high and there was a chandelier hanging over a white marble sculpture of some nymphs. It was two o'clock in the afternoon and even though there was sunshine coming through the windows, there seemed to be more shadows than light. All along the walls were portraits of these old men wearing fancy clothes, whiskers and the expressions I've seen on a lot of pictures of real rich people, like they were surprised by how much they had and surprised, too, that they didn't have even more. Those are the men who founded the school and I could tell they liked what they saw when they looked at what they left behind.

I walked down the long marble hallway, past the highbacked leather chairs and the mahogany tables, and there were more nymphs in every corner. Everything I saw made me feel small. Looked like nothing had ever been touched. Looked like that stuff wasn't even *made* to be touched. Reminded me how my mama used to warn me not to put my hands on anything in the homes of those people she cleaned house for. I always wondered what my hands would do to those mirrors and dishes their hands wouldn't.

And as I got closer to my classroom, I wondered what I could learn in a building like that that was going to save me. Because that's what my mama told me education was supposed to do. Anyway, the feeling I got walking through that building, down those halls, sank into my skin and made me sick. I think I felt that way because I couldn't find anything there that made me think of me. By the time I got to the classroom, my hands were all sweaty and the muscles in my stomach were in knots so tight I almost had cramps. I looked in and saw, over a hundred students. Saw an empty seat for me and not another black face. Then, without even thinking about it, just feeling like this was what I had to do, I turned around and walked back to the entrance. On the way out of the building those old men in whiskers looked down at me again. I knew they didn't see me. And I knew I didn't care.

At night, when I'm walking to the dorm from the library, the buildings on campus look like ghosts. There's so many towers and belfries, I swear, sometimes I hear the voices of people from centuries ago as I'm walking to class. I guess when they built the school they wanted it to look like it had always been here, like Winthrop University had a history, right from the start. Just being here with the buildings that look as old as the trees, so big and gloomy closed in around you and keeping everything else out, I get lost sometimes. Not lost like I don't know where I'm going. But lost like I can't figure out which way to go.

And they're always talking about tradition. My Freshman Composition teacher told the class the first day that we weren't ordinary students. That since we'd been accepted by Winthrop, we were part of a tradition she knew we could all uphold. My adviser keeps telling me if my grades don't improve, it's the school I'll be letting down, even more than myself.

When they start talking like that, I just look off somewhere. I can't even look at them, because it all seems so phony. I guess for them it's real. I guess when they come here, that's what they find. But then most of them bring it with them anyway. And they make me feel like I came empty-handed, because who I am fits me different.

One afternoon I was walking down the stairs behind two professors. One was a woman who's taught at Winthrop for over twenty-five years. They call her the Trojan Horse because she's so tough. She was talking to this younger professor and they were disagreeing about something. I couldn't hear much, but I did hear her say, "Well, we all know this open admissions policy is one grand, misguided experiment. And the result will only be a lowering of our standards, not a rise in theirs."

She said this the way people here say a lot of things, like nobody in their right mind would disagree with them. I thought about what she said for a long time, because I knew she was talking about me. And like I do a lot with things I really feel deep, I kept this to myself. The more I feel something sometimes, the more I keep it in. Didn't even tell Serena, and if I'm going to tell anybody anything, I tell her. Then I figured out on my own that not all of us are supposed to stay here. I've even seen some of the white kids up all night on pills, studying and studying, scared to face their parents if they don't do well. Thinking about all the money it costs to go here, worried it'll be wasted.

13

My mama thinks to succeed at a school like this, all I have to do is study. One time I wrote her a letter and told her there were 11,842 students at Winthrop (Serena got the figure for me), and 341 of them are black. She just wrote me back saying, "White folks always outnumbered you, so stop counting them and start outlearning them." But I keep getting the feeling I'm one of those who's not meant to stay. So now it's real hard for me to believe what my teachers tell me.

I didn't want to come here in the first place. All I really wanted was to marry Charles Murphy. I wanted to marry him because I liked the sound of his voice. I grew up hearing my mama's voice and my sisters' and my mama's women friends. I grew up thinking men were some wonderful reward holding themselves back till women did something to deserve them. The men I saw in my friends' houses came and went like they weren't sure the women were good enough for them. I used to wonder where all the men had gone. Why they didn't love us enough to stay. I never got used to hearing only the voices of women. I never got used to my own house. So I couldn't wait to have a house of my own.

The day we told mama we wanted to get married, she made us feel like love was some kind of sin we were guilty of.

"So just what y'all gonna live on besides love?" she asked.

"I'm getting a job with a mechanic when I graduate, I'll be his assistant," Charles told her.

"Did Faith tell you she got a scholarship to go to a college in Boston?"

Charles kind of hung his head like he'd been slapped.

"Yes ma'am, she did."

"And you actually think you can compete with that?" Mama asked him this like she thought he'd gone crazy.

"But it's not the same thing," I said.

"Tell me how it's different? We're talking about your future either way."

"Do you think you can compete with that?" she asked Charles again. Charles kept trying to sit up straight and look mama in the eyes but he couldn't. Finally he said, "But I can give her something worth even more."

"You men are all alike." Mama laughed. "Think what you can make us feel, whether it's in our hearts or between our legs, is the most important thing. And then when the feeling is gone, you go start it up with somebody new. You just offering my daughter the same old thing. She can look at my life and see how much that's bound to get her."

"But this isn't your life," Charles insisted. "It's Faith's and mine."

"And neither one of you is old enough yet to know what to do with it. She can get married anytime. She don't get a chance to go to a school like Winthrop University every day."

And after that, Charles acted like he was embarrassed around me. I told him we didn't need mama's permission to get married. We could just go on and do it. But he didn't want to anymore. I was mad with mama for a long time. Didn't hardly talk to her. Went to my room to do my homework right after dinner every night, then went straight to bed. I guess the way I was acting hurt her, because one day she said to me, "You think it's Charles I hate. It's not him. It's hard times and struggling. That's what I hate and want you not to have when you're raising your kids."

"And it's my daddy you hate too."

"The daddy you wouldn't even know if you passed him on the street."

"The daddy I'd love anyway."

"The daddy I'll never forgive," she told me, pushing herself away from the dinner table, hard and fast, like my daddy was right there with us and had done something to make her mad. "Get you some education and you won't need no man. A degree will never let you down." She turned around from the sink and stared at me with a look I've seen on her face every day of my life. "A college education won't get up in the middle of the night, hit the door and be gone forever. And I don't know nobody ever regretted having a education. I know plenty women regretted having some man or other in their life."

That's the way mama talked all the time. Ever since I can remember. And it made me scared. I think she was scared, too, but I'm not sure of what. But I got tired of being afraid all the time, of men and myself and my feelings, and I decided I was going to find a way not to be scared. The only way I knew not to be scared was to love somebody. So I started loving Charles and I still do. But he doesn't write or call me anymore and I heard he's seeing some other girl. Now mama says I'm flunking out just to spite her.

For a while, rooming with Serena and Crystal was helping me. When I first met Serena, I couldn't resist her laugh. It's real deep and sounds like a song. I saw a film during Black Arts Week last semester about this famous black man I'd never heard of before, named Paul Robeson. One part of the film showed him singing "Old Man River." I felt that man's voice like something I'd waited to hear all my life. Serena's laugh is like that too. And I like to watch her talk because it's like watching a whole lot of different people appear right before your eyes. She's not afraid to let you know what she thinks, or ask for what she wants. She scares and excites me. Maybe that's why I like being around her, hoping I'll catch whatever it is she's got.

I guess you'd say it's Serena I love but Crystal I'd like to be. Crystal sits sometimes, just watching everybody and everything around her. Then she turns it into a poem. At night, she reads what she's written to us. I close my eyes and the words fill up the room, make me feel something that was there all the time but I just didn't see. Crystal reads her poems and I listen to her and Serena talk about what they mean. Yeah, I'd like to be Crystal just so I could use words like I owned them. So I could make people listen to me.

She's got a whole collection of words. Some I never even heard of. And she uses them like a charm.

I hardly ever go off campus. There's some places in the city I feel like I can't go. I don't mean they wouldn't let me. It'd just be hard and I'd feel out of place. Like South Boston. There's nothing there I want to see, but it'd be nice to be able to go over there if I wanted to. Serena says it's no accident they call it south. It's mostly Irish and if you're black and you go into the neighborhood, I hear they'll make you wish you never came. But it's not like they got a whole lot anybody would want. I mean, from all I ever saw of it, much of it's not a lot better than where most poor and working class people live.

And then I heard one of the white girls who's a junior telling somebody the other day she got an apartment in the North End, where the Italians live, and because she wasn't Italian, she felt so unwelcome, she decided to move back on campus.

Before, when I'd think of Boston, I'd think about the Kennedys and people who were liberal. Now I know that's make believe. Last semester I took an African History course. We read all about the hundreds of tribes and how they spoke different languages and were always fighting each other. I guess that's what everybody is here, a member of a tribe. I sure don't see much difference.

Crystal

THERE is a special language they use for us here. One laden with as much potential for treachery as salvation. "Affirmative Action." "Culturally Deprived." The words chill me. And I suspect them most because I had no hand in shaping them. They were handed us to wear like labels that feel oddly like chains. There are days when the campus strikes me as some alien territory to which I am drawn even as it repulses me. We each measure and choose our steps. Faith hugs the sidelines. Serena charges boldly into the fray. And I stand somewhere in the midst of it all, committed but not certain why. Even after three years here, I don't quite know how to share this with my father. It was he, after all, who urged or rather decided that this is where I should go to college. It was he who told me that Winthrop was "the Promised Land."

"The Negro Schools serve a purpose," he'd announced over dinner one night. "But you can get too comfortable attending them, feel too safe. This world, whatever else it is, isn't safe and you might as well build up your defenses in the man's backyard, where he makes the rules. You'll have to deal with him sooner or later. Sooner just might give you an edge."

"Hell," he'd said with a shake of his head, "you and your brother don't know what an education is, what it means, what people have done to get it." And then he told us for the millionth time, "I'd managed to finish up two years at Fisk when my father died. I was looking forward to being a junior when he had a heart attack. And I didn't see the inside of a classroom for almost three years after that. I quit school and came back to D.C. to get a job to help my mother and sister. We wanted, more than anything else, to keep the house. But things got so bad my mother rented out her room, my sister's room and then mine. And at night I slept on a pallet on the living room floor and we made up a room in the attic for my mother and sister to share. I worked at everything—sold tickets at the Howard Theater for a while, was a busboy. I even used to shine shoes right over there at Union Station. And at night, I read over every book I'd brought home with me from Fisk. Read them like reading was some knack I was scared I might lose if I didn't keep it up. And after all that, we lost the house anyway. That's what killed my mother, losing that house.

"And my sister got married right out of high school. Married some guy she didn't even like, just because he had a steady job. Took me two years to save up the money to go back to school. Then when I graduated from Fisk, I taught in one-room schools all over the South, to the children of sharecroppers for seventy-five dollars a month. Looking at me back then, nobody would've known I'd end up being principal of a high school. Nobody'd have known it but me."

Each narration of this story is rendered by my father like a proverb, the details of which contain a special lesson for everyone. Picking up his fork and attacking his salad, he concluded, "I did okay. Inside the Negro society. When your time comes, there won't be a Negro or a white society. There'll just be a society for us all."

And because of my father's loyalty to the meaning of his life, I don't know how to tell him his prediction may not come true.

19

The idyllic calm of the campus was shattered today by a noontime rally against the Vietnam War. The sun, so self-assured and radiant, filled the air with an atmosphere that was nearly festive as students and faculty addressed the crowd from a podium constructed in front of the library. The microphone was hooked up to two huge speakers that carried their voices all over the campus. The words "genocide," "racist war policies," "quagmire" echoed, circling the campus like the warning of some restless spirit risen from the dead. You could hear the speeches inside the study rooms of the dorms, the strangely singsong chant of "No more war" that sounded like someone's heartbeat, competed with the voices of professors who refused to cancel classes and lectured to half-empty rooms.

It was the biggest rally held so far this spring. There were speakers from MIT and Harvard calculating the cost of the war in terms of dollars and cents, foreign policy, ethics and morality. Winthrop had seemed almost immune to the convulsions of the "real world," so benignly paternalistic is the administration. The school gave in quickly, for the sake of image, to the black students' demand for a separate dormitory and increased financial aid. Barely had we, all thirty-eight of us, marched to the president's office before our posture of defiance was extinguished by the president's willingness to sit down with representatives of our group. The revolution, we say, is just around the corner. But Winthrop will resist, will give in and yet keep its identity intact. Will, in fact, I am sure, re-name us and our revolution.

Today Faith asked me how it feels to be smart. She asked the question, which is as loaded as an M-16, as simply as you ask the time or what the weather is like outside. I told her I didn't know what to say because I don't really *feel* smart.

"Sure you do," she countered, with that gaze of hers that is half-innocent, half-seer. "I can see how smart you are by the way you walk. How you look at people straight on and don't feel like you've got to look away until you want to."

When I still didn't answer her, she said, "I'm sure it feels a lot better than being dumb."

"If you were dumb, Winthrop wouldn't have admitted you or given you a scholarship."

"High school smart isn't college smart," she countered, pushing aside the chemistry notes I'd been going over with her. She stood up and stretched, then walked over to the window and began watering her philodendrons, growing rampant and wild, their vines and leaves twirled around wooden posts. When she watered the plants she touched the leaves the way you stroke the head of a child you love. Looking steadily at the plants but talking to me, she said, "I just wish there was more than one way to learn what it is they want us to know. But it's all got to come out of a book and it's all got to be given back on a piece of paper."

"What alternative do you suggest?"

"I don't know," she said, leaving the window and stretching out on her bed. "I don't know."

She lay on her back, staring at the ceiling, and I thought how doll-like she looked, propped against her pillow. She's virtually flat-chested, having dubbed her tiny breasts "lemon drops," wears a size three dress and weighs one hundred and five pounds. Sometimes when we're walking to class together I feel so awkward beside her because I'm five feet ten. Faith has shrunk psychologically to fit her size, convinced, for whatever reason, that her small physical size is the best emotional size for her too. When I was fourteen, and developed a slouch to camouflage my height, my father nagged me to stand up straight, saying otherwise I wouldn't be seen. One day in exasperation he told me to stand up straight because a man couldn't fall in love with me if he couldn't see me. Then I began to try to stretch into my height.

I thought about height and destiny, if that makes any sense, while I watched Faith. I thought she had fallen asleep when she said, "The only thing I do know is, my mama's gonna be disappointed when they send me home. My com-

21

ing here was really for her. Not me. I'm not sure she'll forgive me."

"You talk as if it's a foregone conclusion."

"It is as far as I'm concerned."

I have never known if my parents' intention was irony or affirmation when they named me Crystal. Me, of the dark dark berryripe skin, my mother's full happy lips and my father's broad nose. Me, whose face resembles nothing so much as some patient, wondering African mask. Irony or affirmation? Why should it matter? Why need I ask? Because I am too much of everything. Too tall. Too dark. Too smart. And I still care too much what others see when they look at me.

"Your skin makes people think of Africa," my aunt told me once. "And that makes folks feel mighty uncomfortable. But you are a pretty black girl and don't mind what *nobody* say." She told me I was lovely, a word black people rarely, if ever, use. She said my face had character and that character was not only strong, it was soft too. I was lovely, she told me, because of the strength of my face. But I wonder, because amidst all the shouting, I am still not sure, if "black is beautiful," does that mean I am too?

When the National Guard shot those black students down at Jackson State College last week, in that protest against the school's administration, Serena sat on the steps of the chapel for seventy-two hours. She fasted and wore a black armband, and a lit candle sat on the ground at her side. Refusing to have anything to do with the protest rally the Black Student Union had organized, she said, "We spend so much time shouting, so much time talking. Nobody ever wants to sit still and think about what they're doing to us and why we can't stop it."

So for three days and nights she camped out on the steps, taking a break only around three o'clock in the afternoon and to shower in the morning. The first night, Faith and I couldn't sleep for worrying that something would happen to her. We could see her from our dormitory window, the candle flickering and Serena, an uneven bundle, unmoving and unperturbed inside her sleeping bag. Faith sat up in bed, her eyes wide and bright as hot coals in the darkness, waiting with me for daylight to come.

"I wonder why nobody tried to make her move off the steps?" she asked.

"I think because the chaplain sympathizes with what she's doing and what she feels. I saw him come out and talk to her this evening for almost half an hour. Then before he stood up to leave, he clasped her hands in his."

"I wish she'd let us sit out there with her."

"So do I. But she said she had to do it alone."

"Why?"

"I don't know. Maybe she doesn't even know. But when it's done, I hope she can tell us."

And even when she came into the room during the day to quickly shower and change her clothes, we didn't know what to say. There was something about her, some iridescent quality that made it impossible to take our eyes off her, even as we held back all the words we felt inside.

The second night we sat up again, not so much because we were worried as because we didn't know what else to do. And that's when Faith said, "I'll bet it didn't take no time to kill those kids. I'll bet it was so fast they didn't even know what was happening. And I'll bet they never once thought that something like that could happen to them. I know I wouldn't. That's the funny thing. Sometimes you can just die in a minute. Die just like your dying was as important as tying your shoes or yawning. Seems like it should take longer, like living does. But maybe it's best that it doesn't. I don't think I could live, thinking my death would be anything other than a surprise."

It was dark in the room and the only thing I could see was the movement of Faith's hands across her face, wiping the tears away from her cheeks. I didn't know what to say. She had really left me nothing to say, and so I just watched her get under the covers and felt myself restless and disturbed. I knew I wouldn't sleep and I knew the only thing left to do was write.

> we are like
> the stones we throw,
> unquenchable
> as our people's thirst
> fists turn pebbles
> into spears
> assassinating certitude
>
> digging for blood,
> we find our own
> feel it clog our throats
> swift and convicted
> like we once were.
>
> death is ordinary
>   fast
> our bodies
>   trampled in retreat . . .
>
> nothing like we had
>   imagined
> we had not imagined
> death
> at all.

And when it was finally over and we could ask Serena what she had seen, she told us she felt like she'd been away a very long time.

"People had very strange reactions to me. Some folks were embarrassed, I could tell that. I felt like I was in another world, separate from everyone. The armband and the candle were a kind of shield that put me on one side and everybody else on the other side. But at the same time, I felt closer to people too.

"Some people stopped and asked me what I was protesting. I told them I wasn't protesting anything. I told them I was affirming everybody's right to live. I got a chance to talk to some people for the first time about an issue they couldn't have dealt with if it was scrawled on a picket sign or chanted in a crowd."

"But weren't you scared sleeping out there at night?" Faith asked.

"No, not really, I felt safer sleeping on the steps of the chapel than I have walking across campus."

"Why'd you do it alone?" I asked.

"I wanted to do something personal and very private for those kids, but I wanted everybody to see it. Just the way everybody saw them die."

Serena

I FEEL a real sense of failure and responsibility because Faith is flunking out. Crystal would groan if she heard me say that. She says I'm an egotist masquerading as a martyr. Sure, I believe in helping others and I'm not ashamed to say it. Everybody's walking around calling each other brother and sister. But when I say it, I mean it. I really feel like that's what we are. And we owe something to each other. Like, the only time I ever see *me* is when I look at Faith or Crystal. So if Faith leaves Winthrop because she can't make it, she's going to take a part of me with her.

I tutor her in math and she seems to understand pretty well in our sessions. But she says something happens in the classroom. And when she has to take a test she nearly falls apart. I thought that maybe if she roomed with us she'd feel a little more secure. But then she kept saying she didn't know how to approach her teachers and that she didn't think they cared whether she passed or failed. I've run out of things to say to her. How can I explain that I know as well as she does that this whole process is more about dollars and cents than real wisdom. That it's really a technique, not the mysterious ritual they make it out to be. How can I tell Faith I know all that, that I'm very skeptical about the pro-

26

cess of which I'm a part and that I still believe in it enough to master it. Even as I say it aloud now, it sounds like I'm describing the behavior of a schizophrenic.

She needs to be at a different kind of school. And then, too, Faith hasn't learned how to be a little bit crazy. She doesn't know almost everything requires that. That's why she's flunking out. It's not because she's dumb. It's because she believes too much and she believes too hard.

When my mother and father came here for Parents' Weekend, my mother asked me if I had met any nice boys. What she really wanted to know is if I'd met anybody I'd like to marry. And the first thing my father said was, "I just don't see what you're learning here that you couldn't have learned at a state school."

"I'm learning to take care of myself," I told him.

"You don't have to go to school to do that."

"But you do have to leave home."

They wanted me to go to school in Detroit, where I'm from. My father thinks Detroit is the greatest place on earth. But that's because he's never been anywhere else. I've been to Canada with my high school senior class and to six cities on the East Coast with the debating team. I put a map of the world on my bedroom wall once and my father just looked at it and said, "I don't know what you're looking for in all those places. It's just about the same all over." His job on the assembly line at General Motors, the house he bought for us when I was three, a Sunday visit to his brothers, a few fishing trips in the summer—that's my old man's universe. I swear I'll die before I make do with just that.

We were sitting in a fancy sandwich shop not far from the campus, one of those places where a cup of coffee costs two dollars and they sell delicate pastries instead of doughnuts and buns. My father looked around at the people reading the New York *Times* and slid his chair closer to my mother.

"How do you get along with the other students?" she asked, looking around curiously, as if trying to decide what she thought of what she saw.

"Okay. Sometimes I feel like an experiment, though. Like I'm here to prove something to everybody, not really to learn. Most of us don't hang out with the white kids so much. We kind of stick to ourselves."

"Now does that make any sense?" my father asked in exasperation. "Come to the school and then want to go back to the days of segregation. Got all the freedom we wanted and don't know what to do with it."

"We're pleased with your grades." My mother smiled, offering the words as she hugged her pocketbook to her chest. "Real pleased."

"You be careful though," my father warned.

"Oh, Leon, what're you complaining about now?" my mother asked, just like they were sitting at home in front of the television.

"You be careful," he said, looking around to see if he had been heard. "Don't think everything you see here is meant for you. I want you to be smart, but don't lose your common sense. And don't forget where you came from."

"Now what makes you think she'd go and do that? These folks don't for one minute let her forget where she came from. now do they, Serena, just tell me, do they?"

"No, mama they don't." She seemed strangely vindicated by my answer, so pleased, in fact, that she began poking my father in the side, saying over and over again, "You see, I told you that."

"And all this political stuff, you just leave it alone."

"But what if it won't leave me alone?"

"You open another book and don't take your eyes off the page," my father said.

"You're not here just for you," my mother told me solemnly, reaching across the table for my hand. "Your father's been on the assembly line at GM for twenty years."

"And proud of it, proud of it. It's a damn good company, too, don't come no better," he interjected defensively.

"But who knows what he'd have done if he'd had a chance to be where you are now. Uh-uh, baby," my mother said, patting my hand. "You got a load on you you don't even see."

She was patting my hand the way she does with those little kids in her day care center, like by patting their hands, the tears will stop, the toy will be found, sleep will come. She's been taking care of those kids so long, her approach to them is in everything else she does. She repeats anything important twice, once very loud, so we can hear her over some din that must ring in her head all the time, and once for emphasis so we'll be sure to understand what she said. And though my father has tried valiantly, I don't think he's ever had the last word.

My mother worries a lot about me settling down with somebody who has a nice job and a degree. She, just like my dad, would prefer any lie to my particular brand of truth. So I tell her about this imaginary boyfriend I've got, this one steady guy, not the five who have shot through my life like lightning bolts the past three years here. She'd have a conniption if she knew one of them was from Ghana and another was Ethiopian, and that right now I'm mostly sleeping around, not letting myself feel anything because I'm scared to get hurt. My mother was still patting my hand and it felt real good, real safe, and she'd said it again, just like I knew she would and I heard the last part of it, "On your shoulders you don't even see."

"You can read everything Frantz Fanon wrote. You can sleep with Mao's Little Red Book underneath your pillow every night. All that's gonna make you is a theoretical revolutionary, sister, you hear what I say? A T-H-E-O-R-E-T-I-C-A-L R-E-V-O-L-U-T-I-O-N-A-R-Y, so busy reading about somebody else's revolution you can't make one of your own."

Randy was telling me this from the top of a ladder I held in place as he hammered the sign ROXBURY FREEDOM SCHOOL on the front door of his house. We'd washed the windows, put up curtains from the Salvation Army, cleaned out the front yard, but still the outside of the house didn't look like much. Looked as forlorn and neglected as most of the triple deckers on this block, where over half the houses are abandoned. The abandoned houses give an air of disaster to the street. And it's as if the very presence of those buildings prevents the others from standing with any dignity.

"Well then why open this school?" I asked him as he climbed down the ladder.

" 'Cause these young brothers and sisters are gonna be studying math and science and economics, all the subjects black folks got a complex about. That's the kind of stuff a revolution is made of. Y'all think a revolution is knowing who Frederick Douglass was. I got a dozen families said they'd send their kids here after school and on Saturdays."

Randy gathered up the nails, the hammer and opened the door. I followed him into the kitchen.

"Why don't you make some sandwiches, there's some cheese and lettuce and tomatoes in the refrigerator," he told me as he washed his hands in the sink. The lint-filled nappy uncombed Afro, the T-shirt with the red black and green liberation flag on it, the Fu Manchu beard, the green eyes and all muscular six feet four of him, and I remembered why I once thought I'd always love him.

"But sometimes when I see everything that's happening, it's hard for me to believe a revolution could happen here," I told him.

"That's 'cause you're a college student at Winthrop University," he said, opening a beer and stretching his legs out before him. "If you were a blood on the street, Serena, you'd think anything was possible. That's why y'all black bourgeois revolutionaries make me laugh, think a revolution's gonna happen on a college campus. There's brothers been in Nam who've come back and gone underground already."

I placed his sandwich before him and sat staring at my own.

"I graduate next year and I don't know what I should do afterwards."

"As fast as things are happening, it might not be up to you to decide. You see that picture in the paper yesterday of those Black Panther Party members they arrested in Philly? Had 'em buck naked, stripped, up against the wall of the alley in back of their headquarters. Front page of the *Globe*, twenty-five black men naked and defenseless as chattel. Now tell me with shit like that going down, you'll even have a choice next year?"

"Those guys that were in Vietnam you mentioned, were they with you there?"

"Some of them."

"Why don't you ever talk about it? I've known you two years. We've had sex, gotten high together, you've lent me money, I've cried on your shoulder but never once have you told me what it was like."

"I can't. Hell, I can't tell nobody. I've spent every day since I got back trying to forget and you want me to remember!"

"I'm sorry."

"I will say this, though—all them brothers talking about 'No Vietnamese ever called me nigger,' well that's 'cause they weren't over there. If they'd shipped their butts to Saigon, they'd have been called nigger and a whole lot more by 'our Third World brothers.' We're the only people in the world seeking solidarity with everybody else before we get our own shit together!"

"But what's a revolution got to do with my old man? My mother? They think they've got the good life."

"So your old man works for GM! You let a serious recession hit this country and he'll be screaming for change too."

"But what will all I've learned at Winthrop mean in the end? How will it make a difference?"

"It won't. It can't. What you're really learning is how to be a sophisticated consumer of middle-class values, ideas and tastes. That degree you'll get just makes you a member of a special club. You pay the dues for the rest of your life."

I've learned more from talking with Randy than almost anything else since I came to Boston. Sometimes when I feel claustrophobic on campus, I come spend a few days with him. But the contradictions between the enclosed world of Winthrop University and the exposed atmosphere of Roxbury are too much for one city to contain. I'm stranded between Winthrop, the choices it offers, and the responsibilities imposed by the Roxburys of the world. Randy says history is moving so fast that it will decide my fate. But I don't feel prepared at this point to do much more than write a footnoted term paper on my destiny. I don't think I'd really know how to claim it, no matter what side I chose.

I just felt like getting on the road going somewhere. And I couldn't think of anyplace better to go than New York. I talked Crystal and Faith into coming with me and I borrowed Randy's car. Made reservations at this el-cheapo hotel on the West Side and the cost of two nights and three days came to almost nothing.

Faith and Crystal slept almost the whole drive down. My old man taught me to drive when I was sixteen and I love the feeling of power, the feeling of control it gives you. One day I'd like to drive all the way to California and then down to Mexico, maybe camp out along the way.

I make up stories about the people in the other cars on the highway, give them problems, histories, even names. This old '57 Chevy, beat up but still rolling, came up beside me. Inside was this black guy and a woman. The guy winks at me and gives me the black power fist and the woman waves. I named them Tina and Richard. They zoomed ahead of me and I turned up the radio louder when they shot past, just because they made me feel so good.

Then I spotted a Day-Glo orange, lime and purple Volkswagen bus in front of me, flowers and animals and slithery things and all kinds of weird shit painted all over it. I could tell it was a car full of hippies. The only reason I'd have wanted to be in that van is for the herb I imagined they were passing around.

Then I saw this man and a woman in a station wagon with two kids in the back. The kids were making scary faces out the back window. And the wife kept turning around, trying to get the kids to stop. I've never, not even as a little girl, had fantasies about weddings and husbands and all that crap. Getting married to somebody strikes me as about the least interesting thing I could do.

By the time we got to Jersey, I could almost *feel* New York, and everybody was driving faster. Even getting through the Holland Tunnel didn't phase me. And when we were finally in the city, it hit me with a rush. It always does. A rush of excitement that promises everything and warns me, just like my old man, not to try to touch it.

Faith

SOON as we got to the hotel, Serena fell on the bed and went to sleep. Said she had some friends in Brooklyn who were giving a party that night and she'd told them we were coming. Crystal took a shower and then went out to visit a museum. After she left, I sat for a while looking out the window onto Central Park. I'd decided I wasn't going to let mama know I was here. Hadn't even called her to tell her I was coming. I'd never done anything like that, something so risky. I mean mama could've walked past the hotel and run right into me—then what would I have said?

Before we left, the school put me on probation. And I was so depressed, I started not to come. Figured I'd just spend the weekend studying. But I knew I'd just be looking at the pages without the words meaning anything. I was embarrassed around Crystal and Serena and didn't want them feeling sorrier for me than I already felt for myself. So I kept saying no, I wasn't coming. Told them that for two days straight. Even after they'd packed their overnight bags. I still told them no. Then Serena opened the closet, took out some things for me, stuffed them in her bag, and just pulled me up out of the chair I was sitting in. I didn't even resist, because I think all the time I'd been saying no, I was hoping she'd make me say yes.

On the way to the party we smoked a joint and that made me relax a little bit. When we were eating dinner, all of a sudden, I got real depressed. Started thinking about my lousy grades and how I hated Winthrop and how far away being happy seemed. How it seemed like this year at Winthrop had been a whole lifetime. How even though Crystal and Serena were only juniors I'd never catch up to them in anything. How it seemed like I'd always, all my life, been wanting things I never ended up getting—like one day to see my daddy. To marry Charles. To leave my mama's house for good. To be sure and proud of myself.

Then I just stopped in the middle of eating the spaghetti that tasted like glue and stared off into space. I wanted to cry, but not there and not in front of Serena and Crystal.

"You okay?" Serena asked me.

"Yeah. I just don't like the food."

"It is pretty bad," she agreed.

"I'm going to get some air," I told her, then went outside and walked around the block. When I got back to the front of the hotel, Crystal was standing there and she said, "You don't have to go with us if you don't want to. I mean, if you don't feel well." She was looking at me and her eyes were telling me a lot more than she was saying.

That's the nice thing about Crystal. In spite of all those special words she knows, sometimes instead of using one of them, she says what she means with the look on her face.

But that look made the tears come and I couldn't help it. She handed me some tissues and said, "Come on, let's walk some more." And we did. I stood next to her looking in store windows along Broadway and listening to her talk about how interesting she thought the city was and how she'd like to come here to live one day. And just like a few minutes before, when her look was what I needed, right then, those words that were real ordinary and that didn't ask me why or pressure me to explain, sort of made me feel better. By the time we got back to the hotel, I still felt the tears a little in my heart, but I didn't feel anymore like I *had* to cry in order to go on living.

The house in Brooklyn was packed with people. And red and blue strobe lights gave everybody's face a strange kind of glow. The music was loud and I felt free in a way that I hadn't felt in a long time. Soon as we came in, Serena went off somewhere in the back with the people who were giving the party and some guy latched on to Crystal and kept dancing with her. For a while, I just stood near the corners, watching people dance. They looked like they were at war when the music was fast and like zombies when the music was slow. Then something came over me and I wanted to dance too. I wanted to be held, to lay my head on some-body's shoulder in the dark. I wanted to close my eyes and wake up and find that I was somebody else. So I started moving around the room, around the dancers, pushing through groups of girls standing together looking at the boys leaning up against the walls. I kept pushing through the crowd, not sure what I was looking for, but sure I'd find it. Then the music and the people got to me and I got thirsty, even a little dizzy. So I stopped at a table where there was wine and sodas and stuff. I was sipping a beer when somebody tapped me on the shoulder. I turned around and he asked me to dance.

He smelled like perspiration and leather. And we were dancing so close, we seemed to have become one person. When the record was over a blue strobe light filled his face with shadows and stars. I looked at him closely but I couldn't figure out, by looking at his face, who he was or what he thought of me. And his face was as empty as I felt.

We danced to another slow record and then went outside and sat on the steps in front of the house. We talked and I can't even remember, now, what we said. But under the streetlight I could see him a lot better than I had inside the house. Maybe people give parties in the dark so everybody can hide who they are. I asked him where he went to school and he said, "Nowhere." Then he said, "You want to go for a ride?" Not like he even really wanted to, but just like he couldn't think of anything better to say.

We drove around for a while, neither of us saying much. All I know is, it just seemed like I couldn't help what I was doing. I didn't want it, but I didn't know how to stop it. In his apartment, he lit up a joint and stretched out on his bed, watching me walk around the cluttered, messy rooms. "Why don't you take off your clothes?" he asked me after a while. I didn't have anything to lose, 'cause I couldn't think of anything I had that I really wanted.

When I had undressed and folded up my things in a neat pile on the floor, I felt his hand between my legs and all of a sudden, I was wet where he touched me. Then I circled my own hands around his. He ran his tongue from the bone at the back of my neck to the base of my spine and I heard myself hissing like a cat. It was like being in my body for the very first time. He was bulging and hard inside his pants, pressing my hands against the outline of his penis. And then he took off his clothes and fell on me. But once I was in his arms, I crawled, in my mind, into a small dark place. And I hid there. I don't think it took more than a few minutes. When it was over, he fell asleep. I never once closed my eyes.

Crystal

ZENITH, the school's literary magazine, published two of my poems in the latest issue. Faith read the poems and observed, "Now your secrets belong to everyone." I'd never thought of writing in quite that way and felt uncomfortable with the idea of total revelation, so I told her, "Not really. Everyone's secrets belong to me."

Faith

My period is ten days late. I've been irregular before but this time I know it's not going to come. I know it when I look inside my panties a dozen times a day to see if there's any blood. And I know it won't come even when over and over I stick my finger between my legs, pull the finger out and see it shiny with mucus and nothing more. I'm more scared, now, than I've ever been of anything. I start crying in the middle of brushing my teeth, or walking to class; even in my sleep. Serena and Crystal keep asking me what's wrong. Asking me like they already know. And I can't find anything to say that I could stand to hear.

And if I am pregnant, I know I couldn't kill it. I could never do that. It would be like killing myself. I wouldn't ever feel right again about anything else I did. Besides, it must be nice to have somebody love you just for yourself and not always trying to make you be who they want you to be. That's the only way I'd think a child could love. It's not till they grow up that they love you the wrong way. But for all those years before, I'd have somebody to love me the way God meant.

Serena

FAITH is pregnant and says she wants to keep the baby. She gets down one time with some guy she doesn't even know and gets caught! I asked her why she wanted to keep the child and she said, "Because it's something that belongs to me. Nobody can take it away from me or do it for me." In a funny way, it's almost like she's found what she wanted. She got a B plus on a pop quiz in statistics the other day and a B on a book report. But her grades were so poor before, it didn't make any difference.

I asked her if she'd enjoyed having sex with that guy and she just stared at me like she didn't know that was a possibility.

"It wasn't about that."

"What was it about?"

"About filling me up. I just felt so empty."

I hugged her when she said that. Then we put our jackets on and took a bus over to the Charles River and we sat there watching people jog and sailboats float on the surface of the water. We just sat there for a while and then I told her, "Lots of times, you know, when I have sex with a guy, it isn't that great."

"And do you feel bad when it's over? Worse than before?"

"Sometimes."

"That's how I felt. Like what I was doing was a punishment. I'd always heard so much about sex. How it was so much magic. How it was so special. And then I found out it's no better and no more beautiful than you are when you do it."

"With me," I told her, "mostly I just want to be held and touched. It's not always as good as I thought it would be, but the touching, the holding part, that's always worth it."

"He didn't even tell me his name," she said quietly.

"Did you ask?"

"Uh-uh," she said, shaking her head vehemently.

"Why not?"

"I don't think I wanted to know it."

"Maybe it's just as well. Knowing his name wouldn't have changed anything."

"I've already thought of a name for the baby, if it's a girl."

"Faith, I don't see how you can do this. Why're you trying to give up everything before you have a chance to get it? What'll you do? You're nineteen years old. How will you support it?"

"I don't want to be me," she shouted. "My baby will turn me into somebody my mama can't try to control. For the first time in my life, there won't be anything she can do."

"So you're having this baby to get back at your mother?"

"I'm going to keep my child to find out who I can be."

Crystal

I CAN'T bear to look at Faith now. For her pregnancy reminds me how easily the body I inhabit and that defines me can become my opponent. She's beginning to show and is afraid to go home but can't stay here much longer. She seems oddly liberated. Yet I feel imprisoned or rather conscious of how friendly, natural impulses *can* imprison, each time I look at her. We're all a little shaken by the news, all of us on the "black floor" of Randall Hall. Some say she's a fool, others that she's brave. I say she's both.

I remember how totally unimpressed I was by sex the first time I did it, three months before I graduated from high school. And I felt nothing much more than fear of getting pregnant. Everything took so long—for James's penis to get hard enough for him to put on the rubber, for me to get wet enough for him to get in me, for him to break through my hymen, which must have been encased in steel, and once he was in me, for it to finally be over. And afterwards, we lay entangled, sweaty and exhausted. But I could feel his heart beating hard and triumphant against my chest. And he was so proud. So pleased that I'd given myself to him to prove something to himself.

Faith told me it was her first time having sex. And yet there is still a virginal quality that clings to her. I think in some sense she will always be a virgin.

Faith is leaving tomorrow, and so this evening Serena and I took her out to dinner at a soup-and-salad place not far from campus. She was more quiet even than usual. I kept trying to decipher signs of change in her but found none. Her large, moonlike gray eyes rested as calmly as ever against her copper colored skin. There was no hint of calamity, no trace of cataclysm in her demeanor.

"We're going to miss you," Serena told her.

"Me too, I'll miss you both." The atmosphere at the table was gloomy so I reminded Faith, "You're not leaving us forever, I mean, we'll call you. We'll keep in touch, even visit."

"And when the baby comes, you'll be godmothers, right?"

"Sure," Serena said with a false smile and a grave voice.

"I'm sure I can do this right. I mean, having a baby is the easiest thing in the world."

The waitress brought our desserts and we ate in silence. Then Faith told me, "Words are easy for someone like you, Crystal. But all I've got is feelings." Before I could respond, she continued. "Maybe you've got too many words and I've got too many feelings." Then she said, "You know what I've always wanted from you? I always wanted to ask if you'd give me copies of some of your poems so I could read them myself, and look for me between the lines."

I promised I would give her the poems and thought as I did, that she did not know how to deceive, had not mastered the ability to lie. Maybe that will be her salvation, I prayed to myself, rather than her downfall.

We walked back to school, Faith in the middle, our arms locked, gossiping, giggling, straining for some perfect peace. And by the time we got back to the dorm, I knew that Faith was merely brave.

Faith

THE day I came back home, the first thing I heard when I came up from the subway was music. The record shop on the corner of 155th Street was playing salsa. Made me feel so good, for a few minutes I just stood in front of the store. Let the music wash over me like I was standing in the rain. I even forgot I had to face mama. Felt good to be home and see the bodega next door to the record shop with its wooden stall stuffed with plantains, mangoes, peppers and yams. And even the smell of hot grease and fried fish from Eddie's Seafood Heaven smelled good and trailed me for two blocks. But when I got close to St. Nicholas Avenue I saw the men. A crowd of them, lounging against parked cars, shooting baskets in the fenced-in playground.

Since I was a kid I've watched them standing on those streets like they owned them. Some days walking past them was easy. Other days it was the hardest thing I had to do. But they watched me grow up. Saw me at eight when mama sent me to the store to buy bread and milk. It was like having a whole bunch of uncles then, standing around guarding the store. Then when I turned sixteen and I'd pass by, they'd shift from one foot to the other, rub their chins or let their hands massage their crotches. And they'd stare at me with a look that was closed, not open like before. I hated passing them then because the way they looked at me made me ashamed of being a girl and scared to one day be a woman.

But when I walked past them today, I just held my suitcase tighter and smiled. They called back, "Hey college, welcome home, professor." And I smiled at each one, because they're the only men I've ever known.

Carrie

I ALMOST cried when she told me. Stood in front of her, looking at me like she didn't know why I was so upset, and almost cried. Didn't speak to her for over a week. That child has stole right out of my grasp everything I'd hoped for since she was born. Of the three girls, she's the only one paid any attention in school. Made good grades and they seemed to come easy. But she's not hungry. Never has been. Not hungry to be somebody. She's just satisfied to be who she is, and from where I stand, that ain't hardly enough. When I did start talking to her again, I asked her what she was trying to prove. She didn't say a word. Didn't answer me at all. "I guess you just don't want nothin'," I told her. Then she says, "I want something. Sure I do. But something you didn't pick out or bully me into choosing." Then I slapped her. Slapped her once, then slapped her again, 'cause she'd never raised her voice at me like that. I pushed her onto the floor and she just laid there, staring up at me, her eyes just burning with hate. And then I *did* cry. 'Cause I don't think I ever hit that child more than once or twice before.

And now every time I come into this room I start grieving. Just look at all this stuff. A bassinet, a wall-high stack of

Pampers, a toy box filled to overflowing, baby blankets, undershirts and nightgowns all over the dresser. She must think motherhood's a fantasy. Looks like she's just worshipping the end of her innocence. Rushing to take on a burden she'll never be able to shed.

I admit I spoiled Faith, spoiled her because she reminded me so much of her daddy, who left me a year after she was born. Faith's got that same can't-quite-pin-down or understand quality he had. I never felt, in all the years of my marriage to Matthew Hamilton, that I ever really knew him. It never could've lasted no way, and it didn't. Matthew, who was happiest playing his trumpet or reading a book, laid beside me in bed all those years and I felt sometimes like he wasn't even there.

The first time I ever saw him, in fact, he was reading a book. I was sitting in Central Park, on a hot August Sunday afternoon. I'd been to church that morning around the corner from the rooming house I lived in in Brooklyn, and then come into Manhattan to visit a girlfriend. But first, I decided to stop by the park and just sit like I did sometimes and not think about a thing.

He was sitting on a bench across from me. And now that I look back on it, I realize that he was why I chose to sit where I did. He was reading a thick, heavy book, the kind that whenever I saw them made me want to open them, although I never did. Because I thought books like that weren't written for people like me. I sat on the bench, watching the couples and children and old people pass by, and found I couldn't keep my eyes off him. He had large, wonderful hands that turned the pages of the book almost as if he didn't want to leave a fingerprint. And after a while, he put the book down beside him and looked up and he smiled at me. His smile was sad, like he didn't believe too much in smiling and it embarrassed him. But I smiled back.

I never did get to Delores's house that day. He introduced himself, saying, "I'm a gentleman and a scholar and you look like a mighty fine lady to me." I'd never heard nobody talk like that, spreading words on the air like soft butter over bread. We talked about the weather and the people in the park and I was more pleased than I could understand when he told me the lavender of my dress looked so nice against my brown skin. He sat beside me gentle as a breeze.

We sat in the park a couple of hours and then he asked if he could take me out to dinner. And although since I'd come to New York from Baltimore three years before I'd never gone out with anybody I hadn't met through a friend or at church, I said yes. He took me to a Chinese restaurant and that's where he told me he was a cook in the Navy during the war and that now he worked in a ball-bearing factory in Queens.

"But what I really am, is a musician," he said. We'd go to clubs in Harlem and Brooklyn on Friday and Saturday nights and he'd bring his trumpet. If the group was one he knew, almost always he'd be invited to come up to the stage. And when I watched him play, I'd feel a little fright and a chill would come over me. 'Cause I knew I could never give him anything like what he found standing on that stage, playing that horn. The music never meant much to me. If I loved it at all, it was because I first loved him.

It wasn't like the church music I'd grown up hearing. Or even the music on the radio. It was the kind of music that just had *his* name on it. I'd have had to find something in me I didn't think I had, to love that music as much as he did. To hear in it what he heard. To want to give up as much as he wanted to, for it.

He used to say I couldn't understand him until I really heard what he was saying with his horn. But I swore that wasn't true. I'd never met nobody who wanted to do so much, who acted like he was supposed to have anything he could think up. And I wanted him all the more at first, because he could do something not a whole lot of people could do.

I was working in the garment district, making blouses.

And he was impressed because I worked so hard, because I did overtime two or three times a week and sewed dresses, even made hats for friends, all to earn extra money.

He asked me once why I was working so hard, what I was saving for. "The future," I told him. "Damn, honey, how much the future gonna cost?" he'd teased me, boxing me lightly on the chin. But I knew that he respected me, probably even more than he loved me, because I was so steady. And so we got married, because when I looked at Matthew Hamilton I thought I had found the future and because he needed, he said, "A woman like you to keep my feet on the ground."

I started getting pregnant almost as soon as the wedding was over. Had Esther and Beth right in a row and then two years later, Faith. He didn't want me to work, had made me quit my job. But after Beth we knew that what he made wasn't enough. But my hard work, that he used to be so proud of, only now caused arguments about who was the boss.

When I went back to work we were able for the first time in a long time to make ends meet. And that's when I started losing him. Got so he just looked sad all the time. Came in one day and said he talked to his boss about a promotion. Said the man told him he wasn't getting promoted nowhere, just 'cause he thought he was so smart, thought he was so big, and all he was, was a nigger. Matthew told me, "I wanted to kill him. Felt my hands ready to do it. Then I thought about you and the girls, and I walked out of the room instead. If I'd hit him, I couldn't feed you all. Since I didn't, I just can't look you in the face." That's really when he left us. He was there but was somewhere else from that day on.

And I didn't know how to reach him. Didn't know what to say, what to do. And it was just like with his music. I'd never really heard it, and now I couldn't hear him. And it was to the horn that he turned after that, when he was in a mood, or just wanted to be left alone. Spent every extra penny on

49

jazz albums, sitting in the living room till two in the morning, playing his horn.

Then one day he decided that's all he wanted to do. I was pregnant with Faith then. One night I was getting ready for bed, putting on my nightgown, and he'd put his trumpet on the bedstand and hugged my waist, resting his head on my stomach. "I got to at least *try* to make it at what I was born to do," he said.

"But what we gonna eat? What will we do? You can't make no money—not no *real* money—with that horn."

"Don't you see, if I had a chance, maybe I could."

"But you can't take no risk like that. We got two kids and another one on the way."

"What you think living is, if it ain't taking a risk? I been working in that factory all these years and ain't no further ahead than when I started."

"At least you get a paycheck at the end of every week."

"There's big money, I hook up with the right people."

"Big money, big money." I laughed at him. "Don't nobody know your name." And I regretted the words soon as I said them. 'Cause he looked at me so hard my breathing nearly stopped. "Maybe not now, but one day they will," he told me, still angry as he rolled his eyes and got under the blanket.

And after that he started staying out almost every night, coming in late, playing with a group he and some friends had started. Then he told me he was going on the road.

"Just like that." I cried, holding my stomach, eight months full with Faith. "Walk out and leave us here. I can't get back to work till after the baby comes."

"I ain't walkin' out. I'm trying to find something better for you and me. For all of us." But all I could see was him gone, following the music wherever it led him.

The next morning I woke up and found three hundred dollars in an envelope and a note from him saying his first stop was Cleveland. The night Faith was born, he was in

Chicago and I hadn't seen him in a month. I wouldn't even speak to him when he called the hospital.

He'd spend two or three weeks on the road and then come home with nothing that I could see to show for the time he'd been away. The little money he brought back and sometimes sent I hated because it hardly helped at all. But even more because he made it doing something, I was now more jealous of than if it had been a woman.

I asked him once what he found on the road, traveling, that he couldn't find staying with us. He told me, "It ain't the traveling, baby, it's the music. And the music is the only way I can keep from being a slave. I play this horn and I'm free. I play this horn and I'm a man." Soon I wouldn't let him touch me, gave him my back when he reached for me in bed. I'd leave the room when he started playing that horn. When he went away he started staying for longer times. Then he stopped calling once a week to check on us. And then he called just one last time, to tell me he didn't think he was coming back.

When he left, I was relieved because I thought I'd finally be able to forgive him. But I didn't forgive him, especially when I looked at the three daughters that I had to take care of by myself. I guess I loved Faith the most because I sensed some gift in her, so like her father's need for music, when I watched her making doll clothes or puppets. And she was the one who asked most often about Matthew and who could make me feel angry and bitter and ashamed all at the same time, because he wasn't there.

Every time I come into this room and see all these things I remember how Matthew held on to his dream as tightly as Faith now holds on to hers. And nobody ever did know his name. I used to go into the record stores and thumb through the jazz albums to see if he was listed as a sideman. I even bought the music magazines. And I never saw no mention of him. But I knew then, like I know now, that he knew his name and that was enough. But to spite me, he named our last child Faith, saying, "I'm naming her that because that's what you ain't got, and she's gonna have, because she's a child of mine." And he was right. He blessed and cursed her with a faith in her own confusion that I can't beat back, no matter what. Always asking where her daddy went, and been following in his footsteps all the time.

Carrie

SHE lost the baby. Lost it in the sixth month. But miracle of miracles, it lived for five days. Even the doctors were surprised it survived that long. Losing that baby depressed her so much I kept a close eye on her to make sure she didn't do nothing crazy. I told her that no matter what I'd said, I was sorry the baby had died. Not until she lost it did I know how much it meant to her. She told me that baby was all she wanted and asked me, just like her world had ended, "Now what do I do?"

I've been trying to make up to Faith for a lot of things. We go grocery shopping together on Friday nights and sometimes to the movies on Saturdays. When she first came home from the hospital all she wanted to do was sit in her room with all that stuff she bought for the baby. Finally I got her to pack it all away.

She was suspicious of me when I first started reaching out, but now I think she's beginning to trust me. We don't do so much talking. Never have, really. I guess it was always me talking and Faith listening. But nowadays, in the evenings sometimes, we just sit on my bed watching TV and eating Chinese food. Not talking really, but it just feels like we are.

One night we were sitting in my room sewing. I was putting a hem on a dress. And she was crocheting a pillow cover. I stopped to rest my fingers and told her, "Thank God I could do more with these hands than just clean up after people."

"Nobody's hands were made only to serve others," she told me.

"That's true, but lots of folks don't know their hands can open a book just as well as a can of beer. These hands kept me sane. Saturday nights when other women be out partying in a dress I made them, I'd be sitting up here, sewing a gown for a christening or a wedding. I was making a little extra money and I wasn't going crazy. Thank God for these hands." Then I looked at my hands like they were made of gold. I saw Faith grinning and asked her in a playful, mad way, "What you laughing at?"

"Nothing, mama, nothing at all."

"You better find something useful to do with your hands, I'll tell you that."

"I know what I want to do with them," she said real slow.

"And what's that?"

"Hold on to somebody."

I started to say she'd better learn to hold on to herself, to trust in and believe in Faith. And it almost came out but I caught myself in time, picked up my needle and started sewing again. Then I just said, "There's nothing wrong with using your hands to do that, honey. I just hope you can find somebody who wants to hold on to you as well."

Crystal

WHEN Faith wrote us about losing the baby, I knew I would have to see her. See her to bear witness to our friendship, to what she had lost and to what she might have gained. Just as when we first learned of her pregnancy, I could not bear to look at her, freed of, or, as she would say, denied her child, I could not wait to see her again. I was eager to see Faith, to discover if she now really knew more than me, about love and men and everything. For I had felt that she was not merely heavy with child but heavy as well with an ultimate knowledge, the kind that waits to ambush all women, when they least expect it. I went to visit Faith, bringing a dozen new poems handwritten in calligraphy on pastel paper. I needed to see Faith to know what might lay in store for me.

When I met her mother, I understood everything. She is a stout woman whose worrying, anxious presence filled the small apartment like a mist. Faith has her mother's large eyes, but because the older woman's gaze was so restless, prowling over my face as I sat before her, I was certain there were many things those eyes could never see. The furniture was plastic covered and modest, and the pictures of Martin Luther King, Jr., Jesus and John F. Kennedy were stationed around the living room like ominous warnings of our inevitable damnation. Sitting in that apartment, I imagined Faith as a child running away from home countless times, or perhaps mastering the art of acquiescence to authority, yet plotting silent insurrections even as she obeyed.

In Faith's room, I gave her the poems, and as I watched her unwrap the package, was surprised to see that the only difference in Faith was that her hair was now longer, thicker, a single fat braid stretching almost to the middle of her back. Whatever weight she had gained during her pregnancy had been shed, and she appeared even thinner than before. She looked at the poems and quickly began to read them. But I stopped her and asked, "How are you?"

"I'm fine. Now, anyway," she said, placing the poems on the corner of the bed. "What about Serena? I thought she was going to come too."

"She sprained her ankle a few days ago and couldn't walk too well on it."

Then we talked as though reliving our lives or remembering some experience that had scathed us and everyone we held dear. But even as we talked, I heard no longing for what she had left behind. Faith is a person of indifference rather than renunciation, so I did not ask her if she would try to return to Winthrop or some other school. That question didn't matter, and her response would not have told me anything, even if Faith at that moment had known the answer, and I could tell she did not.

And after a while, after she had gone into the kitchen and brought us two Cokes, and after I'd read a few of the poems to her and we had talked about them, and when I felt her the way I used to feel her sometimes at Winthrop, terribly close, yet enough outside my grasp to make me always want to reach for her, I asked, "Did it hurt to lose the baby?"

And then she told me everything I wanted to know, revealing in the process that she had not told anyone else, in this way, what she was telling me.

"In my third month, I started dreaming about the baby.

Almost every night. But it had no face. And in all the dreams, it was a body floating in the sky like it was already an angel. Pretty soon, I knew I was going to lose it. Maybe it was what I deserved, for getting down with that boy the way I did, with no feeling. Nothing but my body. Nothing good could've come from that. When I think about it now, I don't even know what I wanted from him, except to forget feeling stupid and like there was nothing I could do right.

"It was a girl, just like I thought it would be. I even gave her a name—Jessica. Mama didn't understand why I wanted to see the baby after it had died. Why I gave it a name even after the doctor told me she probably wouldn't make it. She thought it was morbid because I asked one of the nurses to give me the picture of Jessica I took the day after she was born. Everything was so hard for her—breathing, sleeping, eating. They had her body all covered with tubes and tape. And because she was so small and so sick, I couldn't hold her. So I held the picture I'd taken of her instead. I realized that Jessica would always be my first child and more special than any other child I might have after her. Mama told me one night that I lost Jessica so I could find myself. I don't believe that. It sounds too unfair. Maybe mama's right, but the world I believe in's got room for Jessica and me."

Soon we fell asleep on Faith's bed. I woke up and heard the sound of the television in the living room. Faith lay beside me, sleeping the way her child must have, with a light, musical snoring. I didn't want to wake her. So I went to the living room and told her mother good-bye. On the bus back to Boston, I could not say what lay in store for me, but I now knew what undeniably awaited Faith.

Faith

MAMA wants to know what I'm going to do now. I can't think of nothing I want to do except get whole. A part of me is missing, a part that maybe I never really had. I walk down the street just aching, like there's a big hole where whatever it is that keeps you together is supposed to be. I watch the "stories" on television during the day when mama's at work. And what I see there just makes me feel worse, whole bunch a people got money, nice houses, fancy clothes and still unhappy. I've looked through the books I brought from Winthrop and they're more interesting than TV. Now that I don't *have* to read those books, I can. But even when I finish them, I'm still aching, still longing for something bigger than me to hold on to.

I've been walking around with this feeling so long, I'd almost got used to it. Then last week I ran into this girl I went to high school with on the bus. She was dressed in a long robe, and her head was covered up. We got to talking and she told me she had become a Muslim. Said she did it because she wanted to get closer to God. In high school her name was Sheila; now it's Khalika. Back then she was real smart. I figured she'd gone to college and had probably started a career by now. But she's married and she and her husband are going to Saudi Arabia to live for a while and study Islam. I asked her what she meant by "get closer to God." But her stop was coming up and she wrote her name and phone number on a piece of paper and told me to call her so we could talk.

I been looking at that piece of paper Khalika gave me for almost a month now. I put it in my drawer and now and then I pull it out and just hold it in my hand. Every time I look at it, I remember how funny my heart felt when she said she'd wanted to get closer to God. It was like that feeling I have was being filled up, just by her saying those words. I must've been waiting for somebody to tell me what I was looking for, since I couldn't name it myself.

I called Khalika tonight, and she invited me to come to the mosque with her next Friday. I told her I'd think about it and let her know. If I went I'd be an outsider, the way I always am. And I don't know if I want what she's offering bad enough to let go of what's been holding me. This feeling's not good, but at least I know it. What if I go to the mosque and I don't like what I see or the people don't like me? Then I'd have another disappointment to accept. Maybe I'll just leave things like they are. This way, at least, I can't get hurt any more than I already am.

Khalika called me yesterday, wondering why I didn't call her back. I lied, told her I'd been busy. Then she said she understood what I was going through. Said she used to be afraid to be happy too. We talked almost an hour, and when I hung up, I'd told her I'd meet her at the mosque on Friday.

Aisha

"I BELIEVE there is no God but Allah, and the Prophet Muhammad is his messenger."

Praise be to Allah, Lord of the Worlds
The Beneficent, the Merciful
Owner of the Day of Judgment,
Thee (alone) we worship, Thee (alone) we ask for help.
Show us the straight path
The path of those whom Thou has favored,
Not (the path) of those who earn thine anger
Nor those who go astray.

Now I have something to believe in. And I have a new name. Five times a day I make salat (pray) and I am learning how to get closer to God. I have to wash myself before I make salat. And I feel like I'm coming to Allah with a spirit that each time is new. Islam is everything and everywhere with me, just before dawn when I rise for my first prayer and I witness, before most other people, Allah's gift of another day; at night, before I sleep, when I praise him for sheltering and blessing me during the day that is almost past. And each day I ask,

60

A WOMAN'S PLACE

O Lord separate me from my sins as
You have separated the east and the west
O Lord, cleanse me of my sins as the white robe
is cleansed from dirt
O Lord, wash my sins with water, snow and hail

Sometimes in the afternoon, I go to the mosque to pray.
And when I'm finished, I visit for a little while with Khadija,
the Imam's assistant. She is, after the Imam, the most
knowledgeable person in the mosque about Islam. She's
lent me books to read and loves to tell me stories about the
wives of the Prophet. Like the story of Khadija, his first wife
and the first believer in Islam. Khadija was the employer,
follower and wife of the Prophet. She likes to tell me, too, of
the Prophet's enlightened views on women. That he believed women should be educated. "It's the tradition of the
people that changed the true word of the Prophet," she
says. "When I chose my Muslim name, I chose Khadija
because one day I hope to be half the woman she was."

One afternoon I told her, "Sometimes I feel my faith real
strong. Other times I pray, read the Qur'an and I can't feel a
thing." Khadija pulled the letter she was typing out of the
typewriter and read over it for mistakes. Then she signed it
and put it in an envelope.

"Sister Aisha, you act like the faith was a drug." She
laughed. "It's not just a thing you feel, it's what you are,
what you do."

"Do you ever doubt?" I asked.

"In the beginning there were times when I did. When I
was new and impatient and expecting everything to suddenly be easier just because I was a Muslim."

"I don't know that I expected everything to be easier," I
told her. "But I did expect to be more at peace, more
content. And I am, more than I was before. Seems like the
only people I ever saw at peace were either dead or real old.
I wanted to find a way to be at peace while I was alive and
young."

61

"You chose the right path."

Khadija brought a brown bag from a drawer and offered me half of a tuna sandwich. When I reached for it, she said, "You know, you're about the most interesting person I've met in a long time."

"Who, me?"

"Sure, you. You don't think you're interesting?"

"Not really."

"Well, you are." She narrowed her eyes and gazed at me like she was looking into a crystal ball. "You're the youngest and at the same time oldest, saddest and yet the most hopeful young girl I've met in years."

"Where do you see all that?"

"All over you. These clothes we wear don't hide everything. Have you thought about marriage? I know there's several brothers who'd like to know you better, but you run off so fast after Jummah most of the time, nobody can talk to you."

"I haven't even looked at anybody in that way."

"So I've heard."

"What about you?"

"Aisha, I've got four kids I'm raising by myself. Since my second husband died last year, it's my children and my belief that keep me warm at night. But there's a saying in the Hadith that marriage is half the faith. No woman your age should be alone, Aisha. Islam, more than most other religions, is built on the foundation of the family." She must've sensed me getting nervous because she said, "Now don't go losing courage on me." And she offered me half of an apple. "If you didn't have courage you wouldn't have come into the mosque and asked what you had to do to become a Muslim. If you didn't have courage, you wouldn't have stayed once we told you."

Rasheed

SISTER Khadija told me her name is Aisha. I noticed her the first Jummah she came to. A young girl, a child, really. I'm forty-seven years old—old enough to be her father. And I'm a man. But every time I look at her, she reminds me of myself. That girl is waiting for somebody. I've seen the look she's got on her face, too often on my own. Man or woman, loneliness looks the same. I'm lonely. Have been for a long time. And I'm man enough to say it and hopeful enough to think it won't last too much longer.

The rest of my life is in order. My business is doing well. I'm in good health. I feel at peace with Allah. Yet, I'm alone. Maybe this girl can turn what's now just an existence into something more.

At the end of last week's Jummah, a sudden, hard storm broke and I gave a couple of people a ride home, including her. She was the last one I dropped off. I noticed that while everybody else in the car was talking, she was quiet, not in a distant way but like our voices gave her all she needed. I'd arranged it so she was sitting in front with me. She'd smile now and then, or laugh with her eyes, looking straight at you. We stopped for a red light and I just sat watching her

63

beside me, taking in how that felt. She had turned around in her seat a bit and was watching Malik and Kareem and Sister Khadija talk. She must've felt me staring at her, because she turned away from them and looked at me. And I felt like I'd been blessed. By the time we got to her house it was raining harder than ever. I pulled into a space in front of her apartment. "Thank you for the ride, brother Rasheed," she said as she sat reaching for her umbrella and getting ready to open the door.

"Why don't you wait a few minutes till the rain eases up?" I asked her. "You'll get soaked. Besides, the rain is telling us, stay where you are. Rest. Be still while I replenish the earth." I started wiping off the windshield with my hand. And when I finished I said, "Anyway, it would please me if you'd just sit here beside me for a while. I've been trying that on for size since you got in the car and I like the way it fits." She looked kind of puzzled when I said that. "That's all I want from you," I lied. "Maybe you think I've got no right to ask anything. But Islam gives me the right. I don't know you, sister, but we're not strangers."

And for a while we did just that. Sat in the car watching it rain. The thing I liked about her was the silence didn't bother her. Some women would've got nervous, felt like they had to fill up the quiet with talking. But she just sat beside me not needing more than what we had at that moment—the sound of the rain, the car and each other.

Then I started talking. She made me want to talk. Ever since Khadija introduced me to her, I've been waiting to tell this young girl my story. It'd been so long since a woman had made me feel like talking about anything more than the weather, or something in the news, that I was so excited I was stammering a bit at first. And while I was talking, she got comfortable, folded her skirt neatly over her knees, and leaned a little against the car door. She let her arm rest on the back of the seat. And that just made me talk more. I was just talking about myself. But you'd have thought she was listening to something real important.

I found myself telling her everything. Don't know why; it just came out. Told her about my house in Jamaica, Queens, that I built twenty years ago, and my wife who divorced me when I became a Muslim and how she took my son and daughter to Philadelphia. I even told her about my share-cropper daddy, eight brothers and sisters and my mother who was run over by a drunken redneck one night as she came home from the white family she washed clothes for. "There was too much work, too many babies, too many white folks in their way," I heard myself telling her. "I wonder if they ever had a chance to really know each other."

By the time I finished, the rain had stopped and the sky was filled with gray-white clouds. Aisha rolled down the window and the smell of damp, rain-soaked asphalt filled the car.

I looked at my watch and saw that we'd been sitting there for nearly an hour.

"I don't know why I told you all that," I said, wondering if I'd gone too far, said too much.

"You wouldn't have told me unless it was something you wanted me to know."

"I hope one day you'll tell me about yourself."

"My story will be short. I haven't lived as long as you, or learned as much from what I've done. That's something I'm just now discovering, how to live. That's why I became a Muslim." She sounded so sure, so young when she said that.

"I don't know much about love either," she said quietly. "Except that it gets all mixed up with things that don't have anything to do with it. And that it's awfully hard to find."

"You never know," I told her, turning on the ignition. "It could be looking right at you. Maybe you just have to open your eyes."

Aisha

I'VE been thinking about him all week. Especially all those things he said to me. I sit down to read the Qur'an and instead of the words, I see his face. Wash the dishes and all I'm thinking about is him. He told me about his life like he was preparing me for a new chapter of my own. I'd seen him in the mosque lots of times. His hair and goatee are sprinkled with gray. And he looks kind of old, but he's got an energy that just draws people to him. And after Jummah, the other men are always eager to come up to him, shake his hand and talk. He stands surrounded by the others like he's used to being the center of attention. And I've seen some of the other women, even some of the married ones, look at him like they want him.

But I don't know if I like the way he makes me feel. I'd never talked to him before, but he knows a lot about me. Not about the baby or anything like that. But just about me as a person, as a girl, as a woman. I didn't gather this so much from his words as from the way he looked at me and an understanding I heard in his voice. I wonder if I'd ever be able to keep anything from him, or say no to something he asked me to do.

Rasheed

GUESS I must've scared her away. I offered her a ride home after Jummah, but she walked with some of the other women instead. I've been asking myself since then, why she said no. And if she was saying no to the ride, or no to me. I was surprised how hurt I was. Maybe it's better to be alone after all. Rather than to have love tease you and even before you have it, break your heart.

Aisha

LAST Saturday a group of us drove up to the Catskills to see the fall foliage and pick apples. I started out with the others when we got there. I was dragging a basket beside me, throwing apples into it that I plucked from branches in my reach. It was a beautiful day. The leaves were like a rainbow, filling the sky with a smile. And I felt so happy looking at that that I fell to my knees and said a prayer of thanks. By the time my basket was half full, I stopped to rest against a tree and found that I'd wandered away from the others into a grove at the edge of the orchard. I heard footsteps crackling the leaves and I saw brother Rasheed enter the clearing.

"You lost or hiding?" he asked, not even surprised to see me there.

"A little bit of both," I told him.

His basket was almost full and he placed it on the ground and squatted beside it, idly picking apples from around his feet. I could tell he was looking at the ground to avoid looking at me. We hadn't talked much since that day he drove me home. I've been trying to figure out how to accept the feelings he's stirred up in me. Mostly I've been afraid to accept them, so I ignore them and by doing that, I guess I ignore him too. But it was quiet in the grove and I found myself liking the fact that it was just him and me with only the sun shining through the trees like shooting stars. So I told him, "This reminds me of New England. I used to go to school in Boston. One weekend I went up to New Hampshire and it looked just like this."

He finally looked at me and said, "Boston, that's just a stone's throw away."

"Not really," I told him. "I was a *long* way from home."

"I could tell you're educated. Something about how you carry yourself. How you look at people. What you say, what you don't."

The sun was very bright, and I shielded my eyes with my hand and looked at him.

"I don't know how educated I am. I flunked out."

"You gonna try it again? Go to another school?"

"I don't think so."

"Why not?"

"College isn't what I want right now."

"What do you want?" he asked, real quick and eager.

"That's what I'm trying to find out."

"Come on," he said. "We'd better start back." He hoisted his basket on his shoulder, then put mine on top of his and reached out, for the first time, to take my hand. I gave it to him almost gratefully. It felt awkward, but I liked it. It was very quiet. And occasionally we heard an apple falling to the ground. I wrapped my fingers around his, which were bony and brittle.

"My mother was real disappointed when I failed at that school," I said.

"Were you?"

"Not really. I felt like I'd finally gotten rid of something I didn't understand. And now I can't remember anything I learned while I was there."

"Oh, you learned things," he said, and I could hear him relaxing. "You just haven't decided to use the knowledge yet or to let it use you.

"There was a time I wanted to go to college. Felt like it would make me a better businessman, smarter. Maybe even a better person. I took a couple of courses at night, but I never stuck with it. Seemed like I knew more than the teachers. Maybe not about the subject, but surely about the things that matter most."

"I felt the same way at Winthrop. My teachers knew a lot, but they weren't telling me what I needed to hear."

"What did you want them to tell you?"

"About men and women. About things I could hold on to and not suspect."

"Nobody can teach you that. You learn it on your own."

He had stopped walking and turned to look at me, still holding my hand. His eyes were the color of caramel, and the sun filtering through the red and orange leaves overhead made them, as he watched me, seem to be very happy. We could hear the voices of the others and he said, "You ought to be searching for a different kind of teacher." I could feel his grip on my hand beginning to loosen, but I held his tighter.

"Maybe I'll start looking," I told him, still holding his hand, not even caring if the others saw us. "Maybe I will."

Rasheed

SHE reminds me of my first wife, Lena. Even looks like her and carries herself with that same kind of delicate style. But I wanted Lena because she was a woman; I desire Aisha because she's a child. A child who can neither entrap nor fool me. Who does not know how complex and unreliable love can be. Like Aisha, Lena inspired an openness in me which is not my true nature. I told Lena things I didn't even know I felt. She was five years older. Had been married once before. And I planned to give her everything. So I worked two jobs to earn the money to set up my hardware stores. She made me a father twice, and I was proud, but I only associated the children with christenings and birthdays. I spent so much time working that the passing of their days into years I only witnessed now and then, helping them with homework sometimes and looking in on them when I came home at 2 A.M., or falling asleep as I read them a bedtime story.

And when I had made the money, opened the first store, I looked around and I had lost them. I was unsure around the children. They were uncomfortable with me, didn't know how to accept my affection. Challenged my authority while accepting Lena's because she'd always been there. And she had friends, interests, a promotion on her job, that I knew nothing about. I had been too tired to ask, too obsessed with my business to care. I tried to find an explanation for the emptiness that had sprung up where feelings used to be. But I saw no crime, only her unhappiness.

One of the men I'd known when I worked at the post office had become a Muslim. I was always skeptical about most religions. But one day, out of curiosity, I attended a service with Guy and met his wife and children. The reverence of his wife around him, the obedience of the children impressed me. The order I saw in his family made the chaos of my own seem all the greater. I thought Islam would give me back the family I'd lost. But Lena resisted. Even refused to allow me to take the children to the mosque. I joined the faith anyway, and soon it was over between us.

After we separated, more than once I stopped by her apartment to visit the children and ended up staying the night. Lying in her arms, I told her new secrets, more revealing than the old ones. Then one day I came to the apartment and the landlord told me she'd moved. What did all those words earn me? All the pleas, the confessions? And since then loneliness has lived with me. Took over this house staring at me as I ate dinner alone in the kitchen. Mocked me when I left in the morning or pulled into the driveway at night.

I've heard this house laugh at me as it watched me eat too much then feel depression sink into my spirit and steal my appetite for anything other than grief. And the house has seen me, tongue-tied with the children I no longer knew, when they still used to visit on the weekends before Lena married again. And so I promised myself there would be few words next time. There would be possession and there would be control. I want this house to be filled with all the things I lost. And this time, I'll protect them. I won't let them get away.

Aisha

IN the beginning we used to talk a lot. He asked me to tell him things about myself. But we don't do that so much anymore. It's like he has learned already all he needs to know. I know there won't be any denying him. And he is now as confident of me as he seems of himself. After Jummah he comes to the back of the mosque and gives me a look that asks me to come and stand with him. He squeezes my hand and then just wants me to be near him. Like us standing together completes a picture he has of himself. We don't talk so much like before, but there's a bond between us that maybe makes words unnecessary. The things we do are ordinary, simple things. We signed up with some people in the mosque to take an Arabic class at the Y. We study the Hadith together, at my house. And on Wednesday nights at his house there's a Qur'anic study group. I come early and help him make refreshments. He's assuming something very important about us. So am I. But neither one of us knows how to say what it is.

Rasheed

I TOLD sister Khadija I've been seeing her. And I hinted at how deeply I feel for the girl. Khadija is one of the few women I really respect. She carries herself with dignity, and that's rare these days, even among the women in Islam. I've taken her boys out to the park, the movies or on errands with me, just so they could be around a man. I've spent evenings at her house discussing the Qur'an, people in the mosque and anything under the sun. I thought we were friends. So I was surprised when she let me know she had doubts about my wanting Aisha.

I was sitting in her kitchen watching her wash her daughter's hair in the sink. When I told her, she didn't even look at me, just said, "I knew something was up. Everybody in the mosque does."

"Well, what do you think?"

"Why should it matter, what I think."

"You're right. It shouldn't. But it does." She was drying Amina's hair and trying, I could tell, not to look at me.

"You know me, I do what I want," I said. "But I was just curious. It's not like what you think will change my mind."

"I wish it could," she said, wrapping the towel around

74

Amina's head and telling her to go into her bedroom. "I just have a fearful feeling, that's all."

"Fearful? You act like I'm some madman, somebody with nothing to offer her."

"Calm down . . . Rasheed, calm down." She poured a cup of tea and sat down across from me at the table. One of the things I like about Khadija is, she won't shrink before you. Right or wrong, she stands up for what she believes. But I could tell what was coming, and for the first time since I'd known her, I wished I could sway her.

"You've had so much more experience." She was finally looking at me. "I wonder if you might not ask her for too much. More than she can give."

"What am I asking for but a wife, a family. Not to be alone."

"I know that sounds very simple to you. But depending on how you want her to fulfill all that, it could be harder than it seems."

I got up and looked out the window, just to avoid her stare.

"A man like you, I never understood why none of the other women in the mosque ever attracted you. You been living like a monk, from what I can see."

"Can you believe I was scared? Scared of choosing with my heart instead of my head. I did that the first time around and I'm still paying for it. I never let a woman get too close because I hadn't met anybody I could have on my terms."

"And you think you can have Aisha, as you say, on your terms?"

"I do. And if I didn't know better, I'd almost say you don't want me to be happy."

"Sure I do. It's just that I want Aisha to be happy too."

"And so I can't . . ."

"I'm not saying that. I'm saying you've decided already, what she's got to be, who she's got to become to please you. What'll you do if she can't do it? If she wants to be someone else? She's yet to be tested. How do you know she can make a commitment to the kind of marriage the faith requires?"

"She's got more conviction than lots of people who *live* in the mosque."

"I don't doubt her belief. I just know she's got some growing still to do that's got nothing to do with Allah."

"Everything has to do with Allah."

"You sound like a man who's made up his mind not to listen."

"I sound like a man who's decided what he wants."

"Maybe you're right. Maybe she'll stay the way she is now. But I wouldn't wish that on her or you."

"Anyway, I haven't even asked her yet to be my wife."

"What do you think she'll say?"

"It's been enough just trying to live with the question. I don't yet have the nerve to imagine the answer."

Aisha

HIS house is large. Too big for one person. And in it there are the ghosts of the people who once lived there with him. It's a house that's been lived in too much and too little. All at the same time. Last night after everybody had left to go home after the study group, we were sitting in the kitchen drinking tea. I looked around and thought about the three bedrooms and the study upstairs and the large front and back yards. I thought about all the space in the house and it struck me as maybe not as much of a blessing as it seemed.

So I asked him, "What's it like, to live alone in a big house like this?"

"There are days and nights when it's a pleasure and times when it almost drives me crazy."

"Does it make a difference that you built it?"

"That's why I've stayed in it so long. It's like a second skin."

"I never lived in a house," I told him. "Only apartments. Houses I saw in magazines or on television. My grandmother has a house in the country in Maryland, but it's not anything special."

"I've thought of moving out. But I put too much into it,"

he said. "It meant too much to me, building it with my own hands. This isn't just a house, it's everything I believe in. Everything I am."

"Would you ever sell it?"

"No. Never. I'd rent it out, but it'll always belong to me. Could you live in a house like this?" he asked me.

"Alone or with somebody?"

"Could you live in this house with me?"

"I don't think at this point there's any other place I'd rather live." I reached out to touch his hand, but he stood up real quick and went over to the refrigerator and leaned against it with his hands folded across his chest. He was talking to me but looking at his shoes. And he asked me to marry him like he was asking me to do a favor he was afraid might inconvenience me. "I want a wife and a family I can be sure I won't lose. But I've been alone too long for it to be easy to live with me. You're so young. Just looking at you makes me think about starting all over. Fresh. With no mistakes this time." Finally he looked at me and said, "Maybe that's why I want you. Maybe that's why I'm scared, too, of my own desire. And whether or not it'll give me a second chance."

Aisha

HE didn't say anything about love. When I told mama, she said love wasn't the most important thing in a marriage, that it wasn't even always necessary. She said respect was the thing that mattered most. And anyway, "Just because he didn't say it don't mean he don't feel it," she told me. Then she said, "I don't know nothing about you-all's religion and all that. But he strikes me as a decent man." That's about what I'd expect mama to say. There wasn't too much for me to think about really; it had already been decided. Because I like what he's done with his life. And I want to see what he'll do with mine.

Last night he gave me my dowry. I had asked him for a ring, a prayer rug and a copy of the Qur'an. He brought everything all wrapped up in a box and gave it to me, with mama standing right there watching us. Then he brought out another box from his pocket and opened it. Inside were three gold bracelets. He put them on my wrist and told me I was more beautiful than any jewelry and more precious than any stone, because I was a woman who had submitted herself to the will of Allah. I could feel his hands warm, and though we weren't that close to each other, his body wanting me. The urge just came down on him like a fever, but before that feeling could possess us, he dropped my hand and just said real softly, "I took you as my wife the first day I saw you."

Almost everybody in the mosque came to our wedding. Mama made me a long beautiful dress of lace and silk. And Crystal and Serena came, looking like they didn't quite believe what I was doing, but happy for me anyway. After the Imam talked about the meaning and importance of marriage, he joined my and Rasheed's hands and placed a white handkerchief over them. Then I knew I was Rasheed's wife. Then I knew Allah had answered my prayers.

He tells me, when we make love, that my hands feel like dove feathers against his skin. But it took me a long time to learn how to please him. And I'm still learning. The first few weeks after we got married, I was nervous and shy. He'd have to pull me close to him and guide my hands over his neck, chest, along his thighs and between his legs. After a while, I relaxed and could do it naturally.

I like it when we do the same things to each other together. And he has a strange funny taste. I never did that with anybody before. His skin is warm and salty on my lips and his penis brushes against my teeth, resting on my tongue. And then sometimes he smells a little like antiseptic and the scent fills my nostrils. His hairs get inside my nose while he's pushing harder and harder against the walls of my mouth. When he's real excited his fingertips knead my scalp and hold on to my curls. He starts whimpering and it sounds like a baby getting ready to cry. I want to tell him it hurts and just then he pulls himself out and comes inside me. He lays on me for a while, his breath hot and raspy in my ears, his fingers playing with my hair. Then he rolls onto his side of the bed and pulls me close. This time, just to hold me. Almost all the time, I fall asleep in his arms.

One night I told him about Jessica. We were laying on our

backs, just staring at the ceiling. The dark and the things we had just done made me tell him. And when I did, I said, "I didn't expect to grieve. I didn't think it would hurt so much. I missed that baby just like it was a friend instead of a promise." He squeezed my hand and said, "We'll have babies of our own. Babies for you to love and to ensure I'll never die."

Crystal

MY first public reading this afternoon was a baptism and a discovery. Fifteen people had gathered in the musty, book-lined attic of The Poetry Place, a Village bookstore specializing in collections of verse—ancient and new, classic and commercial. The audience sat on the once stately divans, and armchairs whose deep rich satin colors echoed beneath the dust and dirt. Serena and Aisha and my mother sat directly in front of me. I had asked each one of them to come because I needed each one of them to be there.

"New New York City Poets" is the title of the series of Sunday afternoon readings, and it assumes realities that I am not quite sure of. Am I a New York poet because I now call Manhattan home, or because "the city" has fascinated, confounded and inspired me more than any single entity I've yet to encounter? Do I qualify as a poet, when I have yet to have anything published in the kind of literary journals that would legitimize my work? No matter what the answer to these ruminations, I was the third poet to read in the series.

The poems had been seen by only one other person— Syrian DuBois, a marvelously maternal yet frankly sensual black woman poet whose advanced poetry course I'm attending at Brooklyn College. As I read, the words leaped off the page into the arms of real life, commandeered an entirely new existence, indebted to, but not bound by, their previous life on paper. I was overjoyed because the audience's reactions confirmed that I was indeed touching raw nerves and unhealed wounds. And afterward two young women cornered me to say thank you and to tell me the part of their lives I'd left out.

When it was over, mother took Serena, Aisha and me to dinner. My mother, Ameline Jefferson, has the demeanor of a woman whose early circumstances sought to deny her dignity while simultaneously instilling in her a passion for its acquisition. The neat, obviously expensive hat and the navy blue linen suit, set off by a silk cranberry colored blouse, are her talismans. They inform the world that she is my father's wife. Perhaps she has perfected the art of being a lady because so many of the songs she sang before she met my father were drenched in yearning, despite their sorrow and complaint, to be just that.

Laying her soft leather gloves beside her plate, she settled back comfortably in the booth. I could imagine her ankles perfectly crossed under the table, and the heels of her alligator-skin shoes digging into the thick pile of the carpet. She smiled, as if remembering some minor incident that, whenever she recalled it, conjured emotions once cherished but now as unknown to her as a stranger.

Then she looked at Serena and asked her, "Did Crystal tell you I used to be a singer? She's not the only artist in the family."

"No. Did you ever cut a record?"

"I wasn't that good. And I didn't do it long enough to get that far. I used to sing in clubs in the Midwest and the South —Chicago, Kansas City, Atlanta. I sang a little bit of everything—blues, jazz, pop. Maybe that's why I never made it big—I was singing in too many styles."

83

"Did you make lots of money?" Aisha asked her.

"I wasn't singing for money. I was singing for love. I was on the road all those years singing so I could find somebody to take me home."

"Did you find him?" Aisha pressed on, eagerly as a child waiting to hear the end of her favorite story.

"Well, I met Crystal's father. I was singing in a club in Kansas City and he was there one night with his cousin. After the show he came back to my dressing room and told me, 'Lady, I think I'm in love and I don't want you singing for nobody else but me.' Three months later we were married."

As I listened to my mother tell my friends triumphantly this tale of how she captured my father, winning him like some fairy princess through the power and magic of her songs, I recalled the measure and meaning of my parents' union. My mother found love in the home of a man who changed her resolute, beebop voice to a praise song rendered in the church choir on Sunday mornings or a tune hummed wistfully while preparing dinner. Love that required more than she thought she could give and that delivered her. Love that was too much and never enough. I gathered all this from witnessing my parents.

As their daughter, I was no mere spectator, no faintly curious bystander, but an eyewitness to who and what they had committed themselves to become. My mother spent her childhood and adolescence being shunted among foster homes where she was mostly ignored, rather than abused, more often forgotten than mistreated. Homes where her secrets had not mattered because the people among whom she lived could not imagine one so unlucky as she to be in possession of confidences that she longed to keep and was eager to share.

"Do you ever miss singing professionally?" Serena asked.

"A lot of people loved me when I was a singer. Loved me because my voice made them feel good. I never needed affection from a lot of people, just the right ones. That's a long way of saying no, I don't miss it at all."

A surge of pride throbbed within me as I saw Serena and Aisha watching my mother. I felt lucky and pleased to be her child. Serena sat openly assessing my mother, as if her revelations had confirmed some secret she had long suspected. "So if your mother sang for love, Crystal, after your performance today you've got to tell us why you write."

Nobody had ever asked me that question, and I was momentarily stunned because I'd never even thought to ask myself. So I said the only thing that seemed to make any sense. "I guess I write my poems for the same reason. To find love and affirm it over and over again. My love of myself and all the other people who populate the world my poems create."

"I wish your father had come up with me. To hear your poems and to hear you say that," mother said.

"He says writing offers no security."

"He wants you to be comfortable, to have nice things. So do I."

"But neither of you can name any endeavor we undertake out of passion or need that offers the kind of guarantee you think I deserve."

"Of course we can't. No one can. I'm proud of you; your father is too. We just want you to be practical."

"I think your mother's trying to tell you your poems probably won't pay the rent," Serena said with a rueful smile.

"I know that," I said. "And I also know my writing never lets me forget who or what it's possible for me to be."

> The songs my mother sang
> were unexpected
> substantial
>   melodies,
> unfolding inside men's hearts
> pumped

              suddenly
        full of her.

        Carved into women's ears,
        moon-eyed hungry children
        the mute
                    dry
                        dust of eternity
        sculpted onto their cheeks
                                    straining
        to taste
        what some know
        and never tell

"I like your friends," mother said warmly, sitting before me in the big overstuffed chair she bought me when I moved into this apartment. She cradled her glass, half full of the Courvoisier she had brought with her, for me. As usual, her body was controlled, somewhat closed, even with the cuffs of her blouse rolled up and her shoes resting on their sides before her stockinged feet. My mother appeared ready to call a stockholders meeting to order, rather than to offer an appraisal of my friends.

"They're so different, Serena and Aisha, but now that I've met them I understand perfectly your affection for them."

"Aisha I think of as a small delicate flower, maybe the kind that blooms only at night, or that looks more fragile than it really is," I said. "A flower that's white or pink."

"And Serena?"

"Oh, she's a palm tree, no doubt about that." I laughed. "Tall, commanding, showering largesse and protecting from harm with her sturdy leaves."

"Did you ever want to have both?" I asked, sitting at my mother's feet.

"What do you mean?" She looked at me quizzically, her face appearing almost to panic because of the purposeful vagueness of my question.

86

"Did you ever want to continue singing after you married father?"

She took another sip from her glass and ran her fingers through her mass of solid, silken hair, tinted a reddish brown that makes her light brown skin shimmer. Reluctantly she sighed, as if she had awaited the question for too many years. And now, confronted by it, was unsure of the answer rehearsed for this moment.

"No, I never did."

"Why not?"

"Singing was simply one of the ways I discovered to live. It wasn't what introduced me to my life. And so I could give it up."

"And never look back?"

"Oh, I've looked back. But with less fondness than you may think. There's nothing so glamorous about doing three sets a night in some little out-of-the-way club that's on nobody's map, before an audience that's drunk or so busy talking, they're not listening to you. And because you're dressed the way you are and because your voice gives you a kind of power that people envy and want to possess, all the men think you're for sale. Think you're easy. And sometimes you are. And the only address you have is the car you and your backup musicians call home. I'd been living like that for longer than I want to tell you when your father asked me to marry him."

"Weren't you scared to get married?"

"Yes. I was afraid I wouldn't know how to be a good wife, how to be content in one place, how to be with a man longer than a few months. But I was more afraid of dying on the road, of reaching fifty and singing the same songs for the same audiences, of finding out that all those years I wasn't really any good."

Her denunciation revealed lines pinching the soft skin of her upper lip, and sagged quite suddenly, her chin like an airless balloon. Remembering her past, my mother, for a brief moment, lost her hold on the present.

She turned away from me to place her glass on a nearby table, and when she looked at me again, her face had healed itself and her in an instant. My mother had become, once again, who she had decided to be.

Exhausted by her revelations, she convinced me to take her onto the roof of my building so that we could watch the sun go down. And as we stood watching the sun fade, I heard my mother softly humming "Summertime." She put her arms around my waist and I lay my head against her breast, not feeling at all like a child, but rather like the young woman she had molded in her image and sprinkled with the water of her own dreams.

The sense of the illicit and the dangerous has dissolved in my affair with Ed. It's not as interesting as it once was to be sleeping with a married man. Often I wonder at the source of my attraction to him. Undoubtedly it must have been that, convinced of my own youth and innocence and regarding both as a burden, I looked to him to strip me of them. Once, the hurried, feverish nature of his sexual style was evidence, I felt, that he arrived at my door riveted with desire. Now I understand that he just has to be home by eleven o'clock.

Last night must have established a new world record. In the space of three hours we went to a movie, had dinner, came back here and had sex. I am nearly always unfulfilled by the tentative nature of everything we do when we are together. There is never enough sex, mostly because there is so little time to lie in his arms afterward and allow our bodies to rejoice in the extraordinary event that has just occurred. There is never enough talk because he comes to me most often on his way home to someone with whom he will share the same mundane observations about his day he shares with me. Once he told me that on the days he comes to see me he has to eat two dinners and make love twice.

His calls from the study of his suburban New Jersey home satisfy me more than our in-person conversations. I imagine him leaning back in a swivel chair before his desk, papers he has graded scattered about, an empty coffee mug stationed somewhere before him. He told me his study is in the basement and distanced from the rest of his family, he always sounds a little like he is performing. I cannot figure out, however, for whom. No one could tell that we are lovers by our phone conversations, they are that chaste. How I despise him calling me from his private phone at home—it's just a cheap little macho trick designed to pull a fast one on his wife and to inflate my estimation of his daring. How bold and crazy and satisfied I feel, like I've flown with only the propulsion of my arms, when I call him on that same line at the prearranged times, fearing (?) hoping (?) that his wife (whose name it took him months to tell me) will pick up instead of him.

We inhabit a land filled with more limits than possibilities, more good-byes than hellos. I am always hanging up the phone, watching the clock, waiting for his call, wondering how long he will stay this time, or rubbing my palm over the shadow he leaves on my sheets when he literally jumps out of bed moments after he is through. And yet, because he gave me *The Collected Poems of Gwendolyn Brooks* for my birthday. Because he has a bawdy, infallible sense of humor that I love. Because I do not want to be alone in New York City, he has became a fixture in my life.

Serena and I visited Aisha this afternoon. We hadn't been together, the three of us, in almost two months. To visit Aisha is to enter another universe. Not only because of her religious beliefs but because of the domesticity in which she is entrenched, quite happily it appears, but entrenched nonetheless. I must say that while in her conversion to Islam she has made a choice I could not, she has won my respect by at least making the kind of commitment that I choose to rationalize into meaninglessness. I am too lazy to be an atheist, lack the curiosity and will to study, read and investigate religion and philosophy so that I can stand firmly for or against the existence of God. I am more indifferent than anything else, failing to nurture a relationship with the Supreme Being yet, like a callous, selfish lover, calling on Him when I need Him. And much as I admire Aisha's willingness to make a choice, I'm not yet convinced that what she has done symbolizes courage rather than intellectual and spiritual indolence.

When she first changed her name, out of habit, I still used to call her Faith. And yet she has evolved into Aisha. And I guess it is Aisha anyway that Faith always longed to be.

She welcomes us into her home with a humility that explains everything but informs us of very little. The well-furnished house is kept ruthlessly clean and its white, unadorned walls make it seem almost cavernous. Aisha is heavier now, still carrying weight from her second pregnancy, and her piety makes her seem older. Sometimes I'm unsure whether it is satisfaction or oblivion that I see on her face.

And she seems always surprised to see us, grateful when we call, as if she expected the price of her conversion to be our friendship. Plying us with questions each time, Aisha transforms Serena and me into emissaries from some world of which she has heard rumors that she relies on us to verify or contradict.

After feasting on the lunch of rice, lamb stew and salad and homemade bread Aisha had prepared, we sat in the living room drinking juice and watching the twins playing raucously with a collection of toys.

"I think I'm pregnant," Aisha announced offhandedly, pulling a tissue from her dress pocket, swooping Tariq into her arms and wiping his nose. Tariq sat on her lap, his ethereal two-year-old eyes roaming quizzically from Aisha to Serena to me. The twins bear a striking resemblance to her, duplicating the broad sensuous lips and aquiline nose and even her brows, so thick they look like question marks.

"Are you ready for another so soon?" Serena asked.

"I'm a Muslim woman," Aisha told her with the prideful

ease of the truly convicted. From a corner of the room Tameka began to cry, releasing a loud, passionate wail that momentarily startled us. She was imprisoned beneath a chair and I freed her, retrieving her from the floor.

"I can't imagine myself as a mother. I honestly can't," I said, hugging the child, savoring the smell of talcum powder and baby oil as she lay in my arms sucking her thumb and boxing with the prospect of sleep.

"I never imagined myself as anything else. They weary and restore me," Aisha said. "And I wouldn't have it any other way."

"What scares me is their need—how dependent children are."

"No more than any of us." Aisha shook her head emphatically. "They just express that need without the fear or shame of adults."

"I used to think of them almost as one, simply because they're twins."

"That's because you aren't here to see them all day. There's something solid and incredibly old about Tameka. She's very quiet, and it's like she's saving impressions and conclusions for some moment she chooses to reveal all. She's independent and no-nonsense. Tariq is pure energy unleashed."

"They're so normal. So healthy," Serena observed, then told us, "Don't ever take that for granted. My mother had five miscarriages before she had me. She never talked about how it felt to face death and loss over and over again like that. And I could never imagine what she went through until one evening at dinner when I was home from Winthrop on vacation, I said it was a crime to bring a child into a world as messed up as this one. She got up and came over to where I was sitting and slapped me. Then she went to her bedroom and stayed there the rest of that evening. I was twenty years old and had nearly destroyed her." Serena paused for a moment in which it appeared that she relived that scene in her mind. When she spoke again she said, "I grew up an only child and I received my parents' love and concern in a more direct way because I didn't have to share it. But I could never take a break from their requirements of me."

"I didn't find it so wonderful having two older sisters," Aisha said. "Because they were older they acted like mama when mama wasn't around, and whatever anger they felt toward her, they took out on me. In the summertime mama'd dress me up in a starched frilly dress and Sunday shoes and make me sit outside on the front stoop like I was a doll. I couldn't play with the other kids or I'd get dirty and she'd punish me. She was always telling me she could see I was something special and she wanted me to live up to what she saw in me. But she never said anything like that to my sisters. Then when Esther got pregnant and got married and Beth right after high school moved to live with our aunt in Philadelphia, and hardly ever wrote or called, mama acted surprised. Seems like childhood's nothing more than practice for all the sadness you get when you grow up."

This observation inspired Aisha to hug Tariq, pressing him possessively against her chest and searching his face for signs of discontent.

"If I had children, I wonder when I'd write, how I'd find the time," I asked. "My mother used to do all the things that were important to her after midnight. She was so busy during the day working on her job, then in the evening tending to my father, Brad and me, that the only time she had was then. Sometimes I'd sneak downstairs and see her knitting, or reading, or writing letters. I'd think of her as a thief, stealing the tail end of the day, the hours nobody else wanted or used."

"But she was turning those hours into a fertile time," Serena said pointedly. "Maybe those hours were, for her, not the only time but the best time."

"I haven't given up anything to have the children that was important to me," Aisha told us, setting Tariq on the floor. "I was never one to go out a lot. I never thought there was much for me in the streets. So I don't miss that. And as far as time to myself, I get that when they're napping or when they're asleep. Sure, I'm busy doing other things then around the house, but I feel like even with the kids on my mind, I'm thinking about me."

When Serena and I left Aisha we went to a bar and had a drink. And that was where she told me about her plans to leave the country.

"If we don't get funding to continue the program, I'm gonna take the pennies I've saved and go do something completely unexpected," she announced, sipping the last of a strawberry daiquiri.

"Helping female ex-offenders find decent jobs isn't fashionable anymore. The state of the economy has sapped all the excess guilt and social consciousness we'd been living off of."

"Unexpected like what?"

"I don't know yet."

Serena's hair was cornrowed, the braids symmetrical and thick, traveling in neat lines away from her face. She is still chubby and reflexively hunches her shoulders as if to turn in on herself in an effort to hide her generous breasts.

She covers her body in tentlike caftans, baggy jeans and oversized shirts and sweaters. But despite her efforts to sabotage her sensuality, I've always imagined that men must find her concreteness of body and spirit irresistible. But Serena shrugs this notion off, saying, "It's my tits pure and simple. They get lost in them and then get off pretending they're screwing mama."

"After studying social work at Columbia the most interesting worthwhile job I could find was headquartered in a former grocery store on Flatbush Avenue, working with a group of female ex-offenders everybody has written off."

"Are you so sure there won't be money for next year?"

"It's not just the budget. The low-level jobs the women could get before, just as a way to get started again, aren't so easy to find now."

"So what'll you do if you've no job next year?"

"I was thinking about doing some traveling for a while. Go somewhere and maybe spend a year or two."

"Where?"

"Africa."

"Africa?"

"Sure. What's wrong with that?"

"Nothing, it's just so far."

"You were the one collecting material from Nigeria and Kenya when we were at Winthrop."

"I know. But that was a hobby. You're talking about living there."

"Maybe. I don't know yet."

"What would you do?"

"Whatever needed to be done."

"How can you sit across from me so calmly and talk about going off somewhere you've never been, with no job, no assurance you'll find one?"

"You mean when I could have all that right here?" She laughed.

"You *are* serious."

"Maybe. It's just that I want to test myself. Sometimes I feel no matter how hard I try to work for change here, everything is going to remain the same."

"You think Africa's any different?"

"I know the stakes are higher there and there's more to be done on a basic, elemental level. Maybe I'd feel more useful if the struggle was simpler, if it was about learning to read and how to provide people with clean drinking water."

"You think a complex system of neocolonialism plus tribalism and sexism is easier?"

"Okay, I've oversimplified. All I know is that I need to be part of a process that will at least give me the illusion I've brought about some change."

"But there're other programs here."

"Sure, other Band-Aid, patchwork nonsolutions to problems that aren't really meant to be solved. I just need more than I think I can find here."

"Well, you'll sure have enough work to do there."

"I'm not going just to work. I'm going to find a way to do something that will make a difference."

"So what I do doesn't."

"Sure it does, in the most advanced country on earth. But Crystal, if you ever get a book published, no matter how good it is, half the world couldn't buy it and the other half couldn't read it."

"So poets are irrelevant to the process of social change?"

"I didn't say that."

"Yes you did. You just didn't hear it."

"Are you angry?" she asked timidly.

"A little," I conceded.

"Maybe I'm just jealous. Your source of satisfaction can be seen right before your eyes, every time you write something. It's been so hard to measure what impact we've had on the women in the program. Almost half of them end up back in jail. And the ones who don't, their grip on 'respectability'—a job, no drugs, their own apartment—is always so unsteady, we're afraid that with the first defeat or crisis, they'll find it easier to steal something or to kill somebody again."

"You'll make a difference," I assured Serena. "No matter where you go or what you do. You're too impatient to leave things undisturbed. Poverty and backwardness don't stand a chance in the face of your wrath."

"I'd like to believe that was true."

"In some small, very important way," I told her, "it is."

95

Crystal

I RECEIVED a copy of *Phoenix* in the mail today, the fall issue containing my poem "Full Moon." The magazine is beautifully designed. My poem has been laid out with not just care but affection, enhanced by a black-and-white photo. And yet as I read the poem, I felt cheated. For on the printed page no one could see the erasures, the markouts, the words tested and tossed aside, phrases sculpted and molded, diagnosed and doctored. The poem sat on the page self-satisfied, assured of its completeness. To those who did not know it, the poem said, "I am finished." Yet it whispered to me in another voice, "I never will be."

There are days when I feel like I've been in school all my life. First Winthrop and now Brooklyn College. The master's degree in English I will receive will consign me to the classroom for the rest of my life. While the program at B.C. has been excellent, it is the courses in the Creative Writing Program that have meant the most to me, and especially meeting Syrian DuBois.

I had read her books, heard the literary gossip about her, marveled at how shrouded in myth and near-legend this black woman poet was. Her poems bleed, hold back nothing and surprise with each new reading. I'd bought all her books long before her "establishment" publishers discovered her. I'd even read occasional interviews with her in some of the literary journals. Still none of this prepared me for the woman who has been artist and intellectual provocateur in residence since September. The first class of her advanced poetry seminar, she entered the packed room like a gust of wind. Her black, gray-streaked, curly natural sprouted from her head with the determination of a fiendish halo. And the huge, round silver earrings hung like shields, nearly to her shoulders. The saffron-colored face was freckled and looked at those assembled with eyes that were weary yet curious. She gathered up the folds of the long maroon skirt she wore and sat atop her desk, an impish Buddha, and announced, "My name is Syrian DuBois. By the end of this semester, some of you will know what your name is too."

And then she told us, "I used to stammer when I was a child. It wasn't till I was nineteen, when I started picking up on ideas and believing in myself because I didn't have anything else, that the stammering stopped. I had seven brothers and sisters and I was in the middle. When I was a kid it took me so long to tell people what I wanted, they got tired of listening and figured if I couldn't spit it out, it must not be worth hearing. I started writing poetry when I turned thirty. I hadn't felt or seen anything that could touch me in over two years. I couldn't remember what I'd done the day before and I didn't want to think about what I was going to do tomorrow.

"I'd started stammering again and I had to find a way to spit it out. When I read my poems aloud, I didn't stammer. So. All my poems are written to be read aloud. And everything I write is autobiographical. Everything any writer writes is. You're either writing about your experience, your fantasies, your fears, your nightmares, your secrets, your hopes or the people you're glad you're not or the ones you wonder if you could be. And yes, most of what you've heard about me is true."

"Is Syrian your real name?" a girl shouted from the back.

"I never tell my real name or my age. Neither one has anything to do with who I am."

She liked my work and urged me to expose more of myself in my poetry. "Your readers will never believe anything you write if your language is masked and pretentious," she told the class one afternoon. "If you're ashamed of being human—weak, stupid, as well as God's greatest creation—you'll never be a good poet. Novelists have to love humanity to write anything worthwhile. Poets have to love themselves."

She became my mentor, saying to me once, "You're the only black woman in the class, I've *got* to adopt you." And so, over coffee in the campus restaurant, and in two-hour-long phone conversations, I learned that she ran away from home at sixteen, got married the first time at seventeen, the second time at twenty-four. That she published her own books for several years, designed the covers and had them printed, hawked them at street fairs, conferences and sold them to black bookstores. Once she conducted a poetry marathon, reading for four hours straight on the corner of 125th and Amsterdam Avenue on Malcolm X's birthday. Now she has her own publishing company, called Northstar Press.

We were sitting in a health food restaurant on Sixth Avenue when she told me that she is bisexual.

"And you're also five feet six and you have brown eyes," I said, feeling much less glibness than my words indicated. Feeling, in fact, my hands warm and wet, clutching my fork, praying it did not slip through my fingers.

"How do you feel about that?"

"At this moment, this second, nothing," I told her.

"Good." She smiled, looking at me uncertainly. And of course it did matter, changed everything, so that when she invited me to come to her house for dinner, I almost said no.

And it wasn't until Syrian's tongue was circling my nipple,

after her fingers had fumblingly, too eagerly opened my blouse and her nails were digging into the skin on my arms, not until all that happened, did I tell her to stop. I cannot say that I had not expected her action. Maybe I had longed for it, if only to see what I would do. Of course she didn't stop when I asked her politely, primly, as if I was asking her to pass me the butter rather than that she stop making wet sticky loops with her tongue along my abdomen. My body was rigid, stiff with dread, excitement and fear. I think she mistook the pounding of my heart for arousal, instead of the strangest, most complete kind of erogenous terror I have ever felt. And even when I pushed her away, she gazed back at me, her eyes brimming with the patience one bestows on a naughty but not totally incorrigible child.

"What're you scared of?"

I laughed out loud at how predictable and even ordinary the question was.

"You a virgin?" she wisecracked, fluffing her hair, smoothing over the wrinkles in her skirt, her cheeks slightly flushed.

"You sound just like a man," I observed, feeling my body relax, returning to my proprietorship.

"You're acting just like a woman."

She sat next to me, reconstructing her composure so deftly that it appeared never to have been shattered.

"What made you think I wanted you?" I asked.

"Nothing in particular."

"Then why?"

"Maybe you didn't know how to show it. It turned out I was wrong. I could've been right."

"I don't know if I wanted you. I only know I'm afraid to find out. You're an outlaw. I crave legitimacy too much."

"If you discovered you wanted me, who knows what other exciting things you might unearth?" she said, letting her hand rest on my arm possessively.

"I don't want to look that deep inside. I don't need to be that free."

"I just want to assure you that I don't try to seduce all my protégées, only the ones I really like," she said.

"I'm flattered and reassured," I told her.

"I'm disappointed."

Rasheed

I NEVER get tired of looking at her when she's pregnant. Her skin starts to glow around the fifth month and for the whole time her eyes sparkle. When she is carrying my child and I make love to her, her body's filled with surprises. It becomes the body of the woman she's going to be one day.

I'm a father now, really for the first time. With Tameka and Tariq, we'd both get up at night to feed them. Aisha from her breast. Me with a bottle of her milk. At first I was so amazed we had twins, I didn't know what to do, where to begin, which child to look at, or hold. The first month, I let Randolph run the stores for me, and I stayed home with Aisha. I'd waited so long to have children in this house again I didn't even mind that for weeks seemed like all I smelled was dirty diapers and sour milk, or that me and Carrie kept up the house while Aisha dealt with the babies. None of that bothered me at all. Because I'd missed even this with my other kids. I got so good I could change diapers in a flash, and even feed them without being scared they'd choke. When they started crawling and getting into things, Aisha was always telling them no, taking things out of their hands. But I told her to leave them alone, let them have the run of the house as long as they didn't touch nothing that could hurt them. I'd just sit and watch them. They'd be pulling down magazines from the bottom shelves of the bookcases and knocking over trashcans and squealing every time they found out a new thing to do. I could see my children growing right before my eyes.

I don't much care whether this child is a girl or a boy. Everybody says from the way Aisha's carrying it, that it's a girl. If it is, one of her names will be Rose, that of my mother, to ensure that she's got the same kind of strength she had. We didn't have much, not sharecropping in Macon, Georgia. And it was the kind of life guaranteed you'd never have nothing either. But my mother'd bring home old magazines from the house of the people she worked for. *The Saturday Evening Post* especially. Almost every night we'd look through the magazine after dinner, and looking at those pictures was better than any fairy tale. Mama'd always tell us, "Just 'cause you don't see your face here, don't mean your name ain't on these cars and houses and clothes. There's good things waiting for you to come and claim 'em. Got your name on 'em right now. Always look farther," she told us, "than you can see." And the older I get the more important I think names are. That's why I told Aisha we'll give each of the children one name that comes out of our faith and another name of someone in the family. Those are the two most important things, and without one or the other you don't have very much, in this life or the next.

Aisha

THE houses on our street are well-tended and sturdy. The lawns are neat and most of the driveways have two cars, some even three. Christmastime, everybody's house but ours is dressed up in lights, wreaths and holly. It's as if the people inside were surprised that they had gotten through another year and wanted everybody to know they could afford the year to come. Everybody knows Rasheed, he's lived in the neighborhood so long. When we first got married, the other women on the block were kind of distant. They'd stare at me, not even trying to hide their curiosity. I think they were trying to figure out how young I really am. Then when I had the twins, they became friendlier, stopping to talk when they passed me on the street or saw me at the shopping center with the babies in the double stroller. Seems like a child can win over anybody.

Some of our neighbors are from the islands—Trinidad, Jamaica, Haiti. I've seen pictures of those places and I can't imagine ever wanting to leave them. But Rasheed told me that the islands, despite their beauty, had betrayed the people, given them lives that were meager and secondhand. We were in his study and he pointed to the Caribbean on his globe. He told me about the history of that part of the world, about slavery and sugar cane and the British and the French revolutions. And why all the people think about America when they want to flee.

In the afternoons I put the twins in bed for a nap and after they've gone to sleep I tiptoe back into the room and just look at them sleeping. I study them best when they're asleep, see things about them that I can't when they're laughing or crying. In sleep they don't resist me. And I never look at them long or hard enough to see everything they are.

Today Serena came over to tell me she's going to Africa next month, and that she might stay for a while. She said that she envied me because, as she put it, I had "defined my borders narrowly but found in them a whole world." She sounded excited and a little scared. Her voice had an urgent sound, and she was talking real fast, the way she always does when she's got a plan or has made up her mind to do something. She told me about the closing of the center where she'd been working and said that even if it hadn't run out of funds, she'd probably have left.

"I'd done what I came there to do," she said. "I helped some women who needed training and jobs find both, gave them support and encouragement and met some people I'll never forget. But it wasn't enough. I wanted to do something more. I wonder if I'll ever find a job or an endeavor big enough for me." She talked about wanting to learn French and maybe Swahili while she's in Africa and maybe work with some UN project and go to see Victoria Falls. Just listening to her talk made my heart beat a little faster, made me smile for no reason, made me think maybe I could do anything I wanted to.

It was nice outside so we took the kids into the backyard and put them in the swings. Serena looked around the yard, at the two huge oak trees and the screened-in patio. The air smelled like October—crisp and cold and maybe even snow. "This is so perfect," she said.

"And it's too small for you," I told her.

"Some people have to leave everything they know to discover who they are," she said, giving Tariq a hard push in his swing.

"I don't think you ever leave everything you are," I told her. "Maybe you didn't pack it in your suitcases but believe me it's right there with you." Serena looked at me like she didn't expect me to say something like that and I told her, "There's nights when I still hear my mama giving me a lecture about why I have to go to college. And warning me to trust myself before any man. And sometimes I think about Jessica, especially when I see how healthy the twins are. You know, I've even thought about that boy who made me pregnant? Wondered what he was doing, where he is, and if he's found as much peace as I have. The past never lets you go, never sets you free," I told her. "One way or another you're going to bump into it, trip over it or feel it like a shadow." I pushed Tameka and said, "Remember when I told you that time at Winthrop that I didn't like who I was, that's why I wanted to keep the baby. Now I can see I was so young then, I thought that girl was who I'd always be."

We pushed the kids in the swings a few more minutes and then went inside. We drank hot cider, and even though all Serena was talking about was leaving I didn't feel sad, or like I'd miss her. She left around four o'clock and I couldn't figure out why I felt so happy, so excited the next couple of days. I felt so good, even when I thought about not seeing her for a long time. Then I realized that it was because she'd left behind a little spark of her imagination, a little bit of her courage for me to live on while she's gone.

We named the baby Malika Rose. She was born right in this house, in the same bed where she was conceived. Sister Khadija is a midwife and during the pregnancy she had me drinking special teas for anything that ailed me. We didn't use any medicines or drugs at all. This time I didn't feel like I was giving myself over to people who didn't really care about me, like when I had the twins in the hospital. This time my baby was born where she's going to live. Rasheed took Tameka and Tariq over to stay with mama during my labor. And when he came back he sat in the bedroom to see his child being born. There were times with this baby I wanted to give up, my labor was so long. And it hurt real bad because we weren't using any drugs.

I kept thinking on the things Sister Khadija had told me to and praying to Allah. I could even see how beautiful my baby's face would be when I finally saw it. But it hurt. It didn't feel like there was much difference in the pains when they came. They were all sharp and long. Hard pains that dug into me and didn't want to let go, that made all the breathing exercises useless. And I didn't want to cry or scream because Rasheed was watching and I wanted him to be proud. And to think I'm strong. He was looking at me with no emotion on his face that I could see. Like he was trying as hard as me to control what he felt.

And then the pains stopped for a while and that was when I cried, because I was so tired and felt like my baby was holding me hostage to pain. The only thing I could see very well or hear was the clock and I knew it had been fifteen hours since my baby started trying to move into this world. Rasheed wiped my forehead with a damp cloth, and because he was so close to me I got to see him clearly and I saw that he'd been crying too. I saw that even as he put a dry towel over the pillow beneath my head and tried to make me more comfortable, tears were streaming down his cheeks. I knew not to say anything. I couldn't even think of what to say if I'd had the strength right then. Maybe I'd have just said thank you. And when Sister Khadija came back into the room, my own tears had dried. And I was ready to bring my baby into the world. And two hours later I did.

Malika Rose is a good baby. She sleeps straight through

the night and has an even, friendly disposition. Rasheed has shown me pictures of his mother, and Malika has her eyes. She's not like some babies who stare and stare and you can't tell if they really see or understand what they're looking at. When Malika Rose looks at you, you know she sees you. And her gaze kind of warms you up. She was chubby and very round when she was first born. Even had a double chin. But now she's slimming down and we can see she's going to be tall. Malika Rose has the eyes of a seer. Maybe that's what she will be.

I like children best when they're babies. I look at them then and think everything is possible. But as they get older, I fear for them and am filled with regrets for all the things they will want and never have, the things they will yearn for and lose before they are in their grasp. Then, too, I'm more confident of myself as mother to a baby than an older child. A baby's needs are so basic. The twins will be four next year. They're moving into a childhood that is a never-ending change. And they are so many different children all at once —just when I feel like I know them, they become strangers quite suddenly again.

Rasheed

I ASKED her to dye my hair the other night. Every time I look in the mirror these days, all I see is gray—in my beard, my mustache, my hair. She asked why I wanted to dye it. Said she thought it was beautiful. "When I was your age I thought gray hair was pretty too," I told her. "But that's 'cause it was on somebody else's head."

She laughed and looked at my hair like it was something she couldn't resist, saying, "Those silver strands make me imagine all the things you've done and seen."

"All I see in the mirror is endings and things I may never get a chance to do," I told her.

"I wanted you *because* you're older than me," she said, all serious and agitated. "Because I thought you'd teach me everything I figured you must know."

Her eyes were pleading in a quiet way. But they didn't stop me from telling her, "I know what I'm doing."

"You want to dye your hair because it makes you think about death."

"That's not true," I said, uncomfortable because she'd read me so well. "Mostly it makes me think about being helpless and needy and pitied the way my father was when he got old. It makes me feel angry, like the day I was in the park with the kids and this woman sits beside me and starts talking about how cute Tariq and Tameka are and then says, 'I've got grandchildren too.' If I dyed my hair maybe I wouldn't feel like every birthday just meant you becoming more of a woman and me becoming less of a man."

"But how will it change anything?"

"I'll feel like maybe I could live long enough to see my children grow up. Like I could live long enough to give you what you desire *and* what you need. Long enough for us to have a life, not just an interlude."

I don't know if she understood everything I said. I mean *really* understood. Understood as deeply as I felt everything I told her. But she must have because she stood up and draped the towel over my shoulders and started rubbing the dye in. I was surprised even to hear myself saying all those things. I'd told her what I'd sworn never to tell anybody. But because she's my wife, she'd know what I felt even if I never said a word.

I showed her the drawings I've done for the next house. It's gonna be another year or two before I start on it but I'm thinking about it now. We're running out of rooms in this house already. And what with us wanting to have another child, we're going to need more space. I've been working on the drawings for the last couple of months, almost every night. I'll be sitting right here in my study and Aisha's over there in the corner feeding Malika Rose or maybe crocheting. She was rocking Malika Rose to sleep on her back when I asked her to look at what I'd done. I explained where everything would be. We talked about how many bedrooms we'd need and then about where I'd build it. We sat up a couple of hours talking about all that. Then I rolled up the drawings and told her I was going to build a house where we could be happy. "I just want a house," she said, "that's big enough for all of us to grow in. Build us a house where our children can become the people we want them to be," she said. "Build us a house where you can be their father and their friend. Where I can be their mother, your wife and anything else I need to be."

Then she said she was tired and was going to bed. It was past midnight. I told her I'd be upstairs soon. But after she left the room I just sat there, afraid to go to bed, terrified of going to sleep because lately I've been having dreams about suddenly dying, or having a heart attack, getting real sick right in the midst of everything I wanted, losing it all before I could really call it mine.

Aisha

IT'S the month of Ramadan and we've been fasting every day from dawn to sunset. For Rasheed and me, this month is a time when we can not only make our faith stronger, but draw closer to people who share our faith. So at least twice a week during Ramadan, he'll invite someone from the mosque over to share the evening prayers with us and the late-night meal that breaks the fast. Last night he invited a young brother named Ahmed and his three wives. I never liked Ahmed much, he's always struck me as someone of little faith. His wives and children are always dressed real shabby. Nobody knows exactly what he does for a living but I've seen him in Times Square selling incense and jewelry. A few months back, his senior wife came over and told Rasheed they were about to be evicted from their apartment because they were two months behind on the rent. Rasheed talked to the Imam and some of the other men and gave Ahmed the money. So I was surprised when Rasheed said he'd invited them over. But I didn't say anything. I figured he must have some purpose in mind.

Rasheed

SOME of these young brothers come into Islam, think it's a game. Think it's a toy they can play with till they get bored with it and move on to something new. This young brother Ahmed's like that. Got three wives and no job. Since I've known him, never had one. And I've never really trusted him since I met him. I think he thought all he had to do was become a Muslim and that'd make him a man. You get some of these young people just join Islam to reject the white man, society, their family, anything they're mad at and don't understand. We got a whole group of people in the mosque now, I know won't be nowhere to be found in a year. So I'd made up my mind I was going to talk to Ahmed. Not so much for him as because of those three young girls he's got living with him.

I refuse to call them his wives 'cause they don't act in no way like wives to him and he don't act like a husband. Seem like the only thing they've given him is an apartment full of kids. They came into the house—the wives, Ahmed and the six kids—and brought that odor that's around them all the time, like they haven't bathed in a month. The kids' noses all runny, faces full of sores, and the women hardly speaking to

112

each other. And Ahmed walking in front of them, strutting like a peacock.

Aisha served everybody tea. I told Tameka and Tariq to take the kids into their room. And then I almost got sick. Ahmed, sitting there spic and span in a new jacket and trousers and his "wives" all covered up in dirty chadras and faded skirts. We prayed and read from the Qur'an, and I could tell none of them had done that in a long time. I was so mad I could hardly keep my mind on the prayers. We finally finished, and Aisha asked Ahmed's wives to come and help her in the kitchen. They didn't get up as a group, but one by one, acting like they weren't sure they'd get up if the others went.

Ahmed just sat there like he didn't even know them. When the women left the room, he said, "Brother Rasheed, I want to thank you for helping me out with that money. I told the Imam when I get back on my feet, I'd pay it back."

Then I just asked him point-blank, "Tell me, what you doing with three wives?"

"I'm taking care of them, providing for them."

"Providing for them? Man, don't you have eyes? Don't you have any pride? How can you look at those women and those children and call yourself a man?"

"Brother Rasheed, everybody gets down on their luck sometimes."

"Don't give me that. I know you, Ahmed."

"You got me wrong, in fact—"

"In fact, the Imam told me you got all your women on welfare under different names and you take the checks and they don't know what you do with the money. Aminata came in and told him that."

"She's lying. We just needed a little help when I lost my job."

"It's always the most irresponsible ones who take the most wives," I said. "Take the Word and turn it into a license to abuse our women. You ever think how much of a man you had to be to have three wives? No, you just thought about how many women's shoulders you'd need to stand on to make you feel big."

"What you so worried about my wives for, anyway?"

"Because you don't." He got mad then, stood up, hunched his shoulders and called the women out of the kitchen, told them he was leaving.

"They're welcome to stay," I told him. He rolled his eyes at me and just looked at those young girls standing in the doorway to the kitchen, one minute looking at him, the next minute looking at me.

"Come on," he shouted. But they didn't move, just stood rooted to the spot.

"You gonna answer for this when you *do* come home," he threatened them.

"We're watching you, Ahmed, everybody in the mosque is. There's nothing you do we won't see. We're the eyes of Allah." Boy nearly ran to the door when I said that, like I'd put a curse on him. His wives had dinner with us and two of them spent the night. I took them home the next day. Aisha told me I shouldn't have got on Ahmed the way I did, not during Ramadan. But I felt there was no better time than during a period when we're all supposed to be striving to be better Muslims. We're responsible to Allah, but he's charged us with being responsible for each other. And he didn't say we'd make a whole lot of friends carrying out that duty.

Crystal

I'VE begun experimenting with haiku in some of my poems. And wrestling with the style ignited an interest in Japanese culture and philosophy. So I enrolled in a class on Japanese Social History at the New School for Social Research. The class is taught by Professor Fujimoto, a historian who came to this country in the late fifties. Barely five feet tall, he has a penchant for striped bow ties and dark somber suits. He carries his leather briefcase, books and papers like sacred instruments. I sit rapt, fascinated by his lectures, and find myself spontaneously composing haiku in the margins of my textbook and next to lecture notes.

Neil

THE first few sessions of the class I couldn't figure her out. She always sat near the back, erect and very very proper. She didn't speak to anybody when she came in, just settled in her seat and opened her notebook. Sometimes she'd light a cigarette while we all waited for Fujimoto to arrive. And she smoked it like she hated herself for being weak enough to have picked up the habit. When she looked around the room, it was with a curiosity that tried to penetrate everything around her and yet remain at a safe distance. She is dark skinned, a deep deep brown that's blemish free and almost perfect. And the colors she wears—gold sweaters, pink scarves, a blazing red silk blouse one night, that made me want to touch her—all appear to be part of some declaration rather than apparel.

Crystal

HIS chin is too prominent, jutting out beneath his lips, giving his face an odd, off-center curvature, sinking his cheeks just a bit and imbuing him, if you look closely, with a look of perpetual hunger. He asked me to join him for a cup of coffee when class was over and I said yes, because he has stared at me so insistently the past three weeks that I felt there was nothing left to hide. As we sat in a booth in a nearby diner, he told me he was an editor with one of the networks and part-time filmmaker and that he was taking the class as part of his research for a documentary about Japanese-Americans.

"In my job I leave a good deal of the facts on the cutting room floor. I rarely even look at television, I'm so aware of how much gets edited out, how manipulative the process is," he said.

"Japanese-Americans, why're you doing a film on them?"

"For the same reason you're taking this class. For the same reason you compose haiku while Fujimoto is lecturing. They're a fascinating people. Actually the documentary is on the internment of the Japanese during World War Two. I'm going to profile three families whose members were interned and examine how that event affected them, then and now."

"Was it necessary to take this class in order to make your film?"

"I felt it was. Making documentaries always involves an element of exploitation. Trying to understand your subject as well as film it may temper a little of that."

He sat before me, obviously pleased to be revealing all this to me. And his desire to give me some part of himself rescued me from the demands of revelation. Freed me to preserve and protect myself from him while feasting on what he chose, quite generously, to present.

"What are the satisfactions for you in all this?"

"The illusion of being fate rather than being at the mercy of it. That's why documentaries are so interesting. They give the viewer the impression they're seeing facts, unexpurgated and intact. But all they're really seeing is my version of someone else's reality. I edit eight months out of the year, documentaries in the news division. The rest of the year I work on my own films. Most of the stuff I edit on my job covers what they call in the business issues, events. That's why in my work I look at the lives of people. I make the kinds of films the networks think aren't profitable."

"But aren't issues and events created by people?"

"Of course. But the logic of the industry says issues make people watch, people don't. Most of my films have been aired in Canada, West Germany. The market for documentaries in this country is fairly limited. I think that's one reason I find making them so intriguing."

"Are you always drawn to endeavors where the odds are against you?"

"Only in the big issues, like love and work."

"You've told me what you do—now tell me who you are," I asked.

"Do you think I'd reveal my hand so soon?"

"Why not? I'm a stranger. The best person you could find to tell everything to. I don't know any of your friends so I can't use your secrets against you. We are mysteries to each other. So your confessions can hardly threaten me."

"I will tell you this much: I've done what women think men never do—I've thought very carefully about the kind of man I want to be and what that will mean for the woman in my life."

I didn't feel quite as lighthearted or snide in the wake of that answer but I could not resist asking, "What kind of woman *do* you want?"

"One who will never tempt me to try to destroy her." Then, almost to prevent my response, he said very quickly, "So tell me who you are?" His black hair framed his face so boldly it made him look like a dark Viking from a grade-school text. The brows were hooded and thick, arched, it appeared, in ever-present concern.

"I am a black woman," I finally said. "Intent on making my place in a world run by men who look like you."

"You just thought that up this minute, I suppose."

"No, I've been working on that definition all my life."

"That's a very impressive evasion," he concluded.

"Not really. It's just one of the ways I defend and discover myself."

He pushed his coffee cup to the side and said, "I thought that's what white men were masters of—defending and discovering."

"Well, all the people they walked over in the process watched them closely and learned how to turn a vice into a virtue."

"Is this how you torture all your victims?" He smiled, settling back against his booth.

"I'm going easy on you," I said and then laughed for no reason I could find. Laughed not at him but at myself as I saw myself reflected somehow on his face.

"Should I apologize?" I asked.

"I'm sure that would be totally out of character," he said.

"How do you know?"

"Because you've told me more than you realize. And I

can't figure out why I want to come back for more." He signaled for the waitress and paid for our coffees and helped me on with my jacket.

We walked to the subway, and as I started down the steps, I told him, "I don't know what to say." He kissed me gently on my forehead and said, "Good," and walked in the other direction.

For the past month, we've sat in the same café one night a week after class and talked. I am aware of the risk, the danger in all this. And facing him in the confines of the booth we share, or walking to the Sixth Avenue subway, I feel a strange headiness, as if by these simple acts I am delving into some part of myself that with one step further will be unraveled forever. He is white. And that disturbs the improvised dance we perform. He is white, a reality that is not as benign as he asserts, and is as dangerous as I assume. I am conscious of myself when with him, as never before. If I dared love him, it would be the easiest and the most difficult task I would ever undertake. Easy because what he represents is supposed to be what everyone wants. Difficult because even if time and everyone else allowed us to throw off the weight of our inheritance, I don't know if I would.

We had dinner tonight in a trendy new restaurant on the Upper West Side. The kind of place I can rarely afford and that he, I could tell, did not particularly enjoy, because of how blatantly it called attention to itself with showcase windows and fancy linen-covered tables outside. "Nobody comes here to eat," he remarked as we were seated. "They come to devour everyone around them." I asked him if he always approached life as if it were a movie.

"I try to," he said. "It's the only approach I've found yet that makes it bearable. So tell me, what will you do when you finish at Brooklyn College?"

"Try to stay out of the system. I'll teach part-time, do readings, be a writer in residence wherever I can, beg the state, the city, anybody for money so I can devote as much time as possible to writing poems. And if nothing else works, I'll get a typing job to pay the rent. My father is utterly confused by how I have chosen to make use of his investment in my education; confused and, I know, a little betrayed. If I end up teaching full-time, which despite my protestations is quite likely, he will be very proud. But as noble as teaching is, I would prefer somehow to make the time to be a student of life forever."

"What makes you think you can't work a regular job and be, as you say, a student of life?"

"The demands of working full-time in any job blind you after a while to anything that's not directly in front of your face. That's why you take off four months of each year, I assume. To get some distance from everything and to see it all up close."

"You will be formidable in the classroom, I can tell. How are you in love?"

"Formidable."

"I thought so. Anyway, will you meet me halfway?"

The challenge and longing in his voice provoked the same feeling of exposure that tends to hover over me when we are together. The feeling I'd have if someone read my diary or accused me of some transgression I had toyed with but had lacked the courage to commit. He looked at me steadily and then raised his glass of bourbon and asked the question again. I raised my glass of white wine and told him, "I will try."

And so, last night he slept in my canopied bed. We slept finally, around 3 A.M., and I lay next to him wondering what I had done. When he woke up, the room was flooded with a nearly relentless sunlight. He watched me. I assessed him. We were more surprised, I think, than affirmed by each other's presence. He coughed his morning smoker's cough —harsh, dredged from deep inside his lungs, seeming to promise early death. When he recovered, I asked him about his name.

"Bogaert, what kind of name is that?"

"It's Belgian. My father is Belgian and my mother is Jewish."

"That's an interesting mélange."

"I come from a long line of wanderers. My old man's brother lives in South Africa, of all places. I wanted to visit the country once, to see it for myself. But I don't know how much what I'd witness there would inform or free me. I'm afraid it would just taint me."

He rolled over on top of me, his beard prickling my chin, his lean muscular body a weight anchoring me beneath him. And the face I looked into was both innocent and guilty. Yet the generous eyes, at that moment a turbulent dark gray, unlike the calm, plaintive color they assume when he is sure of himself, searched for realms inside me I had never dared to approach.

"Do you ever forgive? Can you ever forget?" he asked, nuzzling my ears and chin with his nose.

"No one ever does either."

"I hope you don't really believe that."

"Of course I do."

"You're saying you won't let me love you."

"I'm saying I don't know how to stop you."

He retreated, choosing to answer me with a kiss, as unsettled as the story I'd watched in his eyes. And my resistance sparked some spirit within him, for he was suddenly, all of him, each muscle, poised and impatient. And I acquiesced, asked no more questions, gave myself to him silently and completely, glad for the cessation of our voices.

Neil

SHE'S so defensive, instinctively shielding herself
from casual, automatic abuse. And I am as helpless as she to
protect her from paying an awful price for what she is. I
didn't make the world. And she can't accept it. Yet I want
her. . . . I want her because she belongs too much to herself to submit fully to anyone.

Crystal

HIS calls from Los Angeles are full of anguish and discovery. The film crew follows the three Japanese families around almost nonstop, documenting generations of changes and continuity. In the Yashika family, the oldest son is a professor at Berkeley; the grandfather talks for hours with Neil about the internment camps, losing property, home, savings. Neil is perpetually exhausted and excited, keyed up and overwrought from eighteen-hour days. He sent me a ticket to come out for a week. A week during which he's going to suspend filming. But I got a call from City College and they want me to teach two courses starting soon, and the Poets in the Schools program of PS 185 in the Bronx has me for another month.

He is back and his days are still long now, with editing nine hours of film into two. The Public Broadcasting System wants to air the film in March. Some days when I leave school I go to the studios where he oversees the editing. I bring in cups of coffee and sit watching the often-argumentative negotiations between him and his editor. It is a laborious and painful process that I comprehend on a basic level but don't fully understand. He has slept on a small cot in the editing suites for the past three nights. And as he asked me to, I brought a change of clothes from his apartment.

Around six o'clock he took a break and went into the bathroom, showered and changed into the clothes I'd brought him. Then we walked over to Ninth Avenue to get some Chinese food.

"How is it going?" I asked once we had settled into a booth. "It's hard to tell just from watching."

"We're behind, but we'll meet our deadline somehow. He's the editor, so he has one perspective. But I wrote the script and directed it, so I've got another. I wanted to oversee the editing because this is the last film on which I'm going to try to do so much."

Picking up a menu, he asked, "Think you could make a film?"

"I don't think so."

"Why not?"

"It's not that I couldn't. I wouldn't want to because I'd have to trust too many people not to betray my idea. When I sit down to write I only have to trust myself, and that's daunting enough."

"I don't see it that way," he said pointedly. "I just have to find a group of people who share my vision. You see it as trust. I call it sharing. Why do you always take such a circumscribed view of things?" he asked in exasperation, stationing his menu before his face and between us.

"Is that a real question or a rhetorical flourish?"

"Don't play games with me now. I'm too tired," he said, rubbing his temples. "All I can deal with at the moment is the kind of conversation *most* people have, not a mental tournament.

"Making a documentary is mostly a very uncomfortable process. I have to invade people's lives with objectivity and compassion, and that's a difficult combination to balance."

"You sound like you don't enjoy what you do."

"I haven't really come to terms with the contradictions of

it. I had to listen to those people tell me all the details of their internment with an ear for the best quotes, not necessarily the truth."

"Are you satisfied with it? Will it be a good film?"

"I don't know. And by the time you find out, it's too late."

I saw two hardy slivers of gray threading through his hair that had sprung up, I knew, in the wake of his work on this film. And even in the brooding silence he imposed I heard again the hoarseness of his voice, nearly cracking with fatigue as we talked. When our orders arrived, he ate quickly, with machinelike thoroughness. Finished, he looked at his watch, glanced in dismay at my half-full plate and said, "I've got to get back."

"Don't work through the night again. Come over to my apartment. Sleep in a real bed. You look awful."

"I never sleep when I'm with you."

"You will tonight. I only want to watch you sleep. Nothing more, promise."

He stood up, looked at the check and tossed a twenty-dollar bill on the table.

"I can't promise. I'm up against the wall."

"I'm twenty minutes away by subway."

"I won't be through till around one."

"You've got a key."

"Maybe," he said, leaning over to kiss me.

On his way out he stopped at the counter and bought a pack of cigarettes and then walked out the door. I saw him crazily dodge traffic as he crossed the street and I knew he would come.

At twelve-thirty I closed the collection of short stories by Colette I was reading, because I heard his key in the door. I heard him rummage through the refrigerator, pour a glass of milk and then I heard the glass being put in the sink. He came into the bedroom, winked at me, undressed and got into the bed and turned out the light. I lay next to him and with a cat's eyes watched him sleep.

A WOMAN'S PLACE

The Netherlands

there were only
a few million
natives to
contend with
in 1652
at Africa's southern tip
"bushmen"
"kaffirs"
the language of destruction
easily fills
the mouth
when you do not know
what to call
what you refuse
to understand

it took
guns
cunning
and force
but finally
they claimed the land
and legislated
its inhabitants
out of existence

what has this to do
with my white lover

love is more dangerous
than hate

this the racists
nazis
fascists
the ordinary cowards
afraid to protest
but not afraid
to follow

A WOMAN'S PLACE

know and
never forget

i am no continent
pillaged
crippled
crawling into the 21st century
labeled
like damaged goods
"third world"
he is neither
greedy
nor cruel
spreading discontent
calling it progress

i am a woman
surprised
and yearning

he is a country
i never
want to leave

Crystal

WHEN I told Aisha about Neil she merely asked, "Is he a good man?" The charity of her response caught me unawares and I roughly replied, "How do I know? He cares for me, has a sensitivity I think is special, but how do I know what that means ultimately?"

"I remember when I met Rasheed," she mused gently. "I had to figure out what I saw when I looked at him. Mama had told my sister Beth about him and she asked me why I wanted a man as old as Rasheed. I knew he was old enough to be my father. Knew there'd be some things he'd give me and some things he'd deny, because of that. But when I looked at him I didn't see an old man. I just saw an answer to a prayer I hadn't heard myself whisper."

"But Rasheed isn't white."

"Don't get in your own way, Crystal. Don't try so hard to understand what's happening to you. I think you're afraid to fall in love."

"Why should I be?"

"You can't dissect it, analyze it, put it on a piece of paper and then type it up."

I looked at Aisha, embarrassed and flattered that she had accumulated such a precise knowledge of me. And then I remembered that friendship is nothing more, really, than that.

"Love makes you wonder rather than know," she said. "You have to face up to being its prisoner as long as it will let you. And there aren't always words to say what it means. There don't always have to be."

"Is that how you feel about Rasheed?"

"For a long time I only knew I had to be with him. It's only just now, in the past year, that I could say I loved him."

"So now are you happy?"

"I don't believe anymore that's what being with someone is about. I don't know if I'm happy. I just know we've made something together that, so far, we can survive and that serves us."

"You make it sound so simple, so easy."

"Then you haven't heard a word I said. Giving myself over to Rasheed has been the hardest thing I've ever done. But I wanted him and I didn't have any choice. And I don't think I could've done much better even if I had."

"Neil asked me one day if I would ever forgive or forget. I told him I could do neither."

"Do you think you're strong enough to go the distance with him?"

"I don't know what the distance is. I don't know if he would lead, aid or abandon me—if we tried to go so far."

"What do you think? Don't give me a lecture, give me an answer," Aisha said.

"I think, if I wanted him, if he proved necessary, I could go farther than the distance. But I don't know what I'd have to do in order to reach it."

The letter from Serena lay on the desk in the room Neil helped me turn into a study. It has been months since I last heard from her. So I removed my shoes, settled comfortably on the sofa and slit the seal.

A WOMAN'S PLACE

Dear Crystal,

Kano is hot, dry and ancient, completely different from the southern part of Nigeria. Despite the fact that the northern section of the country is more populous, because of the rambling, unending openness of the desertlike land you don't feel crowded. After the madness of Lagos, Kano is a joy. The major influence here of course is Islam and I've enclosed several pictures of the mosques. Forward them on to Aisha. The call to worship resounds throughout the city several times a day like some primeval chant, and men gather at the nearest mosque, women reverently kneel on mats spread on the floors of kitchens or bedrooms. Most of the women are in purdah and they only come out at night, walking through the streets cloaked in long veils that in the darkness make them seem like a flock of surreal invading birds. Several weeks ago I attended the opening ceremonies for a new university with the black American couple I am staying with. The university is partially endowed by Alhaji Ibrahim, a leader in the early post-independence period and a wealthy agri-businessman. After the dedication, there was a reception, and since Denise and Walker knew the Alhaji, they introduced us. Two days later he showed up at their house and invited me to dinner. The next day in the afternoon, he drove me on a tour of the city, to the places only someone who was born here would recognize as special. He has four wives and his children are almost my age.

One night I asked him to tell me what it was like in the early days of independence. He gave me a veritable history of the country up to the present. When he finished his account, which was as dramatic as anything I'd ever heard, he said, "Nigerians are a people who love the process of making laws and the challenge of breaking them."

And do you know, he likes my body, my big breasts, even my ass which refuses to go away. All 165 pounds of me!!!! When I told him I preferred to undress in the dark, he insisted on removing my clothes himself, with all the lights on. I was embarrassed, and speechless the first time he did it, yet relieved by the appreciation I saw in his eyes as he looked at me sitting on the edge of the bed, my hands trying idiotically to hide everything he saw. He took off his robes and then turned off the lights and in the dark said, "You are a woman, and as you should, you have a woman's body."

A week later I traveled with him to the Ivory Coast to attend an economic development conference. The men who represented twelve West African countries wore three-piece suits, spit-shined shoes, carried briefcases, were dressed in tribal robes. They were well fed and prosperous. France, Britain, and America was stamped all over them. I tried to think of them as servants of the people they represented but couldn't. They looked like politicians caucusing to determine their individual fates.

The women in Abidjan were supremely feminine, their hair neatly braided, their long dresses snug on their bodies. The young ones walked along the streets that are designed like boulevards, past mock-French cafés, looking like dark-skinned gazelles, their heads high and proud. The French women, wives of two- and three-year contract technicians, doctors, engineers, who hold 60% of the jobs requiring a college degree, walked the same streets in sheer see-through dresses.

The Alhaji wants me to remain in Kano. I will for a while longer. But he is used to buying and owning at will, on impulse, because he has the power. I don't want to become just another thing he owns. I don't know when I'll be back stateside. Every morning I wake up like this is where I belong. In your letter you asked me to be your judge. I'm your friend and will offer you no more than that.

You're a black woman beginning to love a white man. You decide if what's happening to you is what you need. I don't envy you. But you are the echo of my own heart and I wish you well.

Love,

Serena.

That night I tried to explain to Neil how much Serena means to me, how much she is missed. When I asked him if he had a best friend, he said, "My mother and now you." I knew that would be his answer. The fleeting, sporadic nature of men's bonds to one another always amazes me. Their ties appear to be purely expedient. I recall my father's reliance on my mother and now Neil's assumption of my loyalty as well as my love. How do women survive being considered superfluous yet claimed as indispensable? The fear that I could not survive being either was why I kept my apartment even after moving in with Neil.

"So you don't trust me," he had accused when I told him I wanted to keep my own place for a while.

"Sometimes you'll have to leave me alone. I can't explain it any other way."

"And what am I supposed to say to that?"

"I don't know. Maybe there's nothing you can say. I hope you can care enough to understand it. And if you feel it's necessary, to forgive me."

I didn't know how to tell my father about Neil, and so for a long time I did not. Mother knew from the beginning. Knew that Neil was white, and told me that was the least interesting thing I'd told her about him. I'd told her that I would tell father myself, wondering even as I made this extraordinary promise, how I would find the words to do it. So, finally, I went home last weekend. It wasn't until my last day that I told my father. I had driven with him to an open, grassy field near our house where he likes to go to practice his golf swing. It had been a good visit. Since I now have my master's degree and have begun teaching, my father no longer looks upon me as some crazy artistic kook. And the irony is that my father wanted, once, to write. That's what he told me, anyway.

"I wanted to be a writer once," he said, "but I decided to just go on and be a teacher when I realized I didn't really enjoy being alone. Writing makes you publicly accountable for every sin, every act of courage. If you think it's just about putting some words together so they sound pretty, you're wrong. And that's why I don't support so much your urge to write. I want you to be free." It was important, I know, for my father as a product of his times not to be vulnerable, so he chose and I can't say that I blame him, to live his life rather than create it.

He is aging with sublime dignity, and whatever physical strength he loses is supplemented, it seems, by an increase in mental vigor. Sometimes I look at him and am convinced he will never die.

I stood beside him in the field, watching him take the clubs out of the trunk. After he'd slammed it closed, I heard myself blurting out, "I've got a new boyfriend. We're living together."

"Well, don't tell me all the details. I don't approve of those kinds of arrangements and your coming to tell me in person won't lessen my disappointment one bit." He'd hoisted the clubs onto his shoulder and was striding onto the field. I walked faster to keep pace with him. Matching him step for step, I said, "He's white."

He didn't say anything, just continued to walk and then stopped abruptly, pulled out the club he wanted, meticulously placed the ball onto the tee, placed himself before it and then swung with a vigor that I had not expected. The ball landed about sixty feet away. He looked at the spot where the ball stood, searching that distant spot for nearly a minute, then he turned to me.

"I didn't raise you for something like that."

"He loves me."

"Hell, white men been loving black women since they first brought us over here. That ain't nothing new."

"I love him."

"That's nothing new either," he said in disgust, placing the iron back in the holder and spitting on the grass, hard and loud as if spitting out an unpleasant taste.

"Just tell me why you chose their side."

"It's not about sides. It's not about choosing." I heard my voice weak and unconvincing.

"You'd better believe it's about choosing. You better believe it's about sides. About choosing sides and being on the right one. Everything is. If we don't choose, we look back and discover a string of accidents, one mistake after another. I wanted you to go through all those doors they finally opened up. I wanted you to understand 'the man' for your own self-defense. I never intended for you to become them."

"Well, I'm through fighting for you, for everybody," I shouted. "I want to belong to me, not you, not us, not them."

"I didn't raise you to be your own woman," he shouted. My father gazed at me as though his words had unlocked some dreaded family secret my actions had forced him to reveal. "Your life don't belong to just you. It belongs to me, your mother, your people. And now you'll turn into somebody no one will recognize or accept."

He stalked angrily back to the car, leaving me standing in the middle of the field. His words shattered the chirping of the birds and the frivolous shouts of children jumping rope across the street. I could never have released all the tears that I felt then, because it would have required the rest of my life. We drove home in silence. At the house I went upstairs to pack my bags and then sat with my mother trying to tell her what my father had said. But I could not tell her because I refused to give a second life to what felt more and more like an evil spell he had cast upon me.

Neil

WHEN she came back from Washington, I felt like I'd lost her. When she told me what happened, I wondered why I hadn't. She took refuge, as she often does, in her writing, sealing herself in the study most evenings, eating very little, hardly speaking to me. I had gotten an assignment to edit a three-hour special on the arms race and was working sixteen-hour days. I was glad to be so busy, happy to flee the guilt her retreat from me inevitably inflicts.

This evening she suddenly got nostalgic. And after dinner when I brought two cups of espresso into the living room, I found her sitting on the floor in the midst of a jumble of albums by Otis Redding, Al Green, Aretha Franklin. Her eyes were closed, she was rocking her body, swaying to the sound of Junior Walker asking with his saxophone, "What Does It Take to Win Your Love for Me?" When she opened her eyes I told her, "I'd take on all your pain if I could. You know that, don't you? But I can only guess how you must feel. And wonder why I have to cost you so much."

I handed her the cup and said with an uncomfortable laugh, "Because I'm not sure that I'm worth all this."

She turned down the volume on the record player and

said, "You're an abstraction to him. If he saw you as a man, just like himself, that would open him up to a host of possibilities he's not ready to accept."

"If he were to meet me now, the only thing he'd see is history, and he couldn't understand why that's not all you see too."

She took a sip from her coffee, and as she placed the cup carefully on the saucer said, "I hate you too sometimes, you know. I told him I only wanted to belong to myself. But I'd give almost anything to belong once again to him."

"I've felt it."

"Do you know why?"

"Because you think I'm getting off scot-free, that none of this is costing me anything."

"Is it costing you?"

"Sure, I'm scared one day you'll look at me and just see what your father does."

"But I don't see that. If I did I wouldn't be here. I couldn't be. He asked me why I'd chosen your side."

"You haven't begun to choose sides yet," I told her. "But the day you do, we're all going to pay."

Crystal asked me if I had always approached life as if it were a movie. I think I often do because that was how, in my family, we survived being with one another. My mother thoroughly mastered the role of the hysterical, victimized housewife, always depressed and agitated. My father was once as charming as he later became ruthless. To protect ourselves, my sister and I evolved, in time, into an audience perfectly tailored to the cinematic poses that substituted for real feeling. And yet knowing all this, I took Crystal to California at Thanksgiving to meet my parents, perhaps because I can't just yet, anyway, meet hers. Yet I didn't approach this journey with as much aplomb as it may seem, for when you introduce your parents to friends or lovers you expose the source of much that you are, and answer questions people are often too polite to ask.

My parents live in La Jolla, where the houses exude the demeanor of their owners—a jaded cheeriness that seems to have exhausted them. My mother met us at the airport wearing layers of makeup that give her face the kind of sullen, totally corrupt youthfulness she cherishes because she's afraid of growing old. As she always does, she hugged me too long, too hard, like I'd returned from combat or had been found, against all odds, alive in the Amazon jungle. And I, as always, let her hold me this way. When she'd finished I held her hand in my palm and looked deep into her eyes to try to find her. Most of the men in my mother's life have encouraged her successful descent into the grip of self-doubt. I'm her only son, so I've always felt I had to try to make up for what the other men did or failed to do.

"And you're Crystal," Carla said, when I released her hand. She hugged Crystal with an enthusiasm that I'm sure Crystal couldn't believe. Standing in the middle of the airport, watching my mother assess Crystal and finally conclude, "You're beautiful, absolutely beautiful," made me cringe. For I knew that Crystal would see only falsity, the liberal accepting California veneer. Crossing the parking lot to the Volvo, Carla asked her, "Is this your first time out here?"

"Yes, it is."

"Your eyes hinted at that. They remind me of how mine must have looked when we first came out here after the war." Carla looked up at the sky and gazed longingly at the palm trees. "I simply couldn't believe it."

When we arrived at the house, Carla took Crystal upstairs to help her get settled and I looked around. I never feel comfortable in my parents' house since it was bought not to provide shelter or comfort, but as a medal my father could wear. I heard my mother's voice from upstairs—frantic, cheery, interrupted now and then by Crystal's thoughtful murmur. I walked over to the glass doors and looked at the backyard, the clay tennis courts and the gazebo that sits a few feet from the court, next to a small pond, the water very still, a film of algae covering its surface.

When I was in high school my father used to bug me all the time to invite kids from school over on the weekends to play tennis. But I didn't have a lot of friends, and the ones I had weren't interested in playing tennis. Neither was I. He wanted to walk around this house and the half-acre that surrounds it like the lord of some eighteenth-century manor, able to look in every room and see the prosperous, happy fruit of his labor. All he saw most of the time was my mother upstairs in their bedroom crying, my sister driving away from the house in a car with some boy, me moving from room to room to avoid him, and himself standing in the middle of that damned tennis court, all dressed up in starched and pressed white shorts and top, hitting balls against the wall all alone.

When my father came in that evening, after dropping his briefcase on the table next to the door, and before speaking to anyone, he headed for the bar. He downed a Scotch and soda, and after pouring a second one, descended the marble steps that lead into the sunken living room and said hello. Loosening his tie, Jacob kissed Carla on the cheek. Caught off guard by the gesture, my mother's eyes gleamed with mockery. A moment later her hands grazed her cheek as if to wipe the kiss away.

Shaking Crystal's hand, my father said, "Welcome to California, young lady. Welcome to our home." Then he sat down possessively beside Carla, but as he stretched his arm out behind her she rose and fled into the kitchen, saying, "Soup's on in a minute."

While I feel that I owe it to my mother to always look at her very closely, I can't look at my father very long. Unlike Carla, who refuses to submit to the embrace of age, my father appears to have aggressively pursued it, unwittingly, of course. It's in the eyes; that's where you see everything. And my father's are surrounded by weak, transparent veins and sturdy crow's-feet. They're flat and dull, like there's nothing more, really, that they want to see.

He took a sip from his drink and over the rim of the glass watched Carla in the kitchen. When he'd finished the drink he turned back to us.

"I saw that film you did on the Japanese on television. Not bad. Kind of interesting. But tell me—who cares? With your talent, you should be making films that millions of people can see."

I'd heard it all before. Every time I come home, in fact, I hear it. So I just sat before my father, pushing my ego into some part of myself out of his reach.

"What's your next project?" he asked.

"I'm thinking about doing a film on Vietnam veterans. I'll go after major funding this time, so I can take some real time off, not just a couple of months."

He shook his head in dismay, sat wordlessly fondling his drink in lieu of offering any judgment. Then he said to Crystal, "Neil tells me you're a poet. I can see the two of you like to live dangerously."

Jacob turned back to me and asked, "But why not come back out here, where real movies are made? The kind of stuff you're doing will get you awards, maybe, but no money." He leaned forward, resting his elbows on his knees, his body steeled, waiting for my answer.

"We don't have to talk about this now, do we?"

"Well, no, we don't. You never listen to my advice anyway."

"What does that have to do with anything?"

"It's got everything to do with everything."

"Can't I ever come into this house and be left alone?"

"If you want to be left alone, stay in New York, damnit."

Going back to the bar, he said, "That's the trouble, always has been. Everybody in this family wanted to be left alone. Nobody wanted to listen, not to me anyway."

"Dad, come on, not now," I pleaded.

"Your girlfriend's got a family. Hell, she knows families aren't like they show them on TV."

He sat on a stool at the bar and looked at Crystal and asked, "Did he tell you I've got friends in the movie business out here who could've opened doors for him? Did he tell you he could've been a big-time director by now? I've made a bundle in real estate. Sold houses to some of the richest people out here. But every chance, every lucky break I offered, he refused. Said he wanted to make it on his own. Nobody makes it on their own, except in the movies."

He chuckled loudly at his observation and then told Crystal, "We go through this every time he comes home. I don't know why I even care. It's his mother he comes to see, not me."

"You've got no right to put me or Crystal through this," I said.

"Rights, rights! Who're you to talk to me about rights?" he shouted. "I have got rights. Maybe you don't respect me, but you have to listen to me. You have to. And I guess she told you we're getting a divorce?" he asked quietly. "I came in one evening last week and she tells me she wants a divorce and the papers are on the dining room table. I asked her why she was doing this and she said so she could stop hating me. She said she had hated me for thirty-five years and now she wanted to stop."

"I told you I'd hated myself for thirty-five years. You just helped me to perfect it." Carla's voice came from the doorway of the kitchen, where she stood, appearing untouched by Jacob's charge.

"Dinner's ready." She smiled, untying her apron. "Let's eat before we all lose our appetites."

"How do you feel about the divorce?" Crystal asked me that night.

"Puzzled. I wonder why it didn't happen years ago. I wonder why bother now. I guess my mother will do well. My father—I don't know."

"What does your sister think about them?"

"She never comes home. She married some guy from India and lives in Calcutta. We hear from her when she has a baby and at Christmas. She swears my mother destroyed our father. I swear just the opposite."

"What's it all about, really?"

"When I was six, my father used to smash his fists through the walls in our house. When I was eight, he stopped hitting the walls and hit my mother instead. By the time I was in high school, the beatings stopped. But by then they had nothing left to say to one another. She wouldn't sleep in the same room with him, was a perfect hostess when we had guests and ignored the old man completely. One night after a dinner party he tried to beat her like in the old days. But she didn't fight back, scream or cry. She told him, 'This time, you'll just have to kill me.' He never touched her again. How do you tally the score in a battle like that? Who the hell can win?"

What I'd just told Crystal unnerved me so much in the remembering and the telling I suddenly put my arms around her and held her very close. But I couldn't stop talking.

"My mother never had any real friends. I don't think she knew how to make them. Instead of friends, she adopted causes. She used to drive to L.A. twice a week to do volunteer work in a drug rehab center. She organized a drive to raise money for some Indian children on a reservation. My father told her once that she loved the world and everybody in it more than she had ever loved him."

"Did he really offer you all those chances like he said?"

"Sure, but I wanted so badly to get away from him—and back then, from my mother too—I went to college in the East. Went East and never looked back. I'd never taken my life seriously out here.

"There was the horror of my parents' marriage and at the same time eternal sunshine and miles of beaches as far as you could drive. None of it made any sense to me. Like the kids I went to school with—one of my best buddies became a clown with Ringling Brothers, another joined some commune out in Wyoming. We didn't grow up to face reality. We hadn't learned how. I spent so much time, as a child, convincing myself that what went on in my house was a dream, I wanted to go somewhere where reality was tangible and unmistakable. That's why I went to New York, studied philosophy at Columbia and then N.Y.U.'s film school. My father never forgave me for turning my back on what he wanted to give me. I felt like I'd end up like them if I stayed out here."

"He loves you very much."

"I've known him all my life and he's never said he loved me, or that he was proud of me."

"It can't possibly be easy for someone like him. He's too uncertain of whether or not he's proud of himself."

Finally I ran out of words. Crystal wanted to make love but I just held her. Anything more would've been too much. Anything less and I might not have made it.

The day before we left for New York, Carla took us to her pottery shop. I'd told Crystal about the time my mother was hospitalized for depression. It was then that she discovered the therapeutic value of pottery. She likes to say it wasn't the drugs but rather the wheel that saved her. She's gotten into sculpture as well. And it is sculptures now that dominate the store. One was a kind of totem pole carved from mahogany, with the faces of women of different races. An Oriental woman, her eyes closed, smiled at the bottom. Above her, a Native American woman stared proudly, a single tear carved into her cheek. A black woman with a full-lipped, ageless face gazed ahead as if hypnotized. On the top of the pole sat a featureless face—smooth, untouched, vacant of eyes, nose, mouth, expression. This void was surrounded by long flowing hair. Crystal stared at the sculpture in silence, walking slowly around it. Her hands were protectively thrust into her jacket pockets, her shoulders hunched as if the sculpture emitted an arctic wind. She circled it half a dozen times before allowing her hands to touch the dark, burnished wood.

"I want to see it with my eyes closed," she announced, shutting her eyes tightly, running her fingers over each woman's face. "It's incredible. I've never seen anything like it," she concluded, as she opened her eyes.

"She says nobody will buy it," I told Crystal.

"It's got too much emotion. Either they don't know what it means and won't buy it, or they do know what it means and won't buy it." Carla laughed.

"Would you want to sell it?" Crystal asked.

"Not really. The reactions I get to it are worth more than anything I'd make on it."

We followed Carla to a back room cluttered with a pottery wheel, mounds of clay and instruments. The whole area was filled with the smell of dust. We stood watching Carla put things in order.

"Why do you even bother with pottery when your sculpture is so strong?" Crystal asked.

"I need what both require. Working with clay, the feel of its texture on my hands, the rhythm of the wheel, shaping it, glazing it—I find that very relaxing. And sculpting lets me release a lot of tension." Carla washed her hands at a small sink and wiped them on a towel. "My analyst says I have to hold on to everything I feel I need. And let go of anything that could harm me."

She must have felt my apprehension, my fear that she might totter, as she used to, over the edge of an invisible but rigorously imposed boundary. For she looked at me and asked, "You don't mind me saying that, do you, Neil? I'm not ashamed of me. Are you?"

"Of course not, mother. I never was. Not ever."

"Let's go outside where it's cooler," she said, opening a door that led out onto a cobblestoned area in the back of the store. It was actually a small garden area. We sat in director's chairs and listened to the whine of BMWs and

Mercedeses along the street and the patter of Papagallo shoes.

"Analysis is rather extreme, isn't it?" Crystal wondered aloud. "I mean, your work is so strong."

"That's only lately. You should've seen the junk in there a year ago," Carla said slowly. "I want my life back. Before it's too late."

"Mother, I'm sure Crystal's not interested," I began, but Crystal silenced me with a look that told me she was. And Carla charged ahead, saying, "You can't imagine what it's like to feel that someone has stolen your life, and to know that you let them do it."

"Do you really think I can't imagine that?" Crystal asked gently.

Carla ignored the question and asked us both, her face suddenly quite young and charming, almost gay, "Do you know what I've always wanted? A happy ending. We were supposed to find one in California. That's really why we came out here you know." She threw her head back and her eyes roamed the sky overhead, as if hoping that one last look might reveal what she sought. And when she looked at us once again, Carla said with no surprise and even less bitterness, "But I haven't seen a rainbow since we arrived."

Crystal

September 10:

I HAVE formed a group with five other poets and we call ourselves Poets Incorporated. The idea is to sponsor readings and workshops around the city and wherever else we can. Our group is unusual for at a time when men and women are moving further and further away from each other in all realms, we are a rather happy cross-sex joint action—three women and three men. And, oddly enough, it is the men's poetry that is tender and longing and the two other women write verse that is declarative and almost frightening in its sense of themselves as *others.* Jonathan Cartwright is a social worker who writes either love poems or verses about the lives of the children he shepherds through the city's juvenile court system. Dayo Oshun is a legal secretary by day who dresses like some modernist painting—long, angular earrings, a style of dress that combines vests with dashikis or long flowing dresses, sandals, a "nose earring" and dreadlocked hair. Her style is polemical, and her poems are elegies for society. I wish she offered more hope than she apparently feels is necessary. Elizabeth Hughes, the other woman in the group, teaches, only rather

147

than doing short stints at colleges part-time or poeting in the public schools for a semester like me, she is a tenured professor at Sarah Lawrence, her alma mater. Her mind is a precision-honed key that smoothly opens any door that might seek to resist her. And her poetry is sleek and smooth, and though her style, personal and poetic, is *cool,* with continued exposure, the internal fire that she stokes and hoards becomes more evident.

Franklin Mojo is funny, effervescent and irreverent, a "performance poet" who bares his soul like a talking diary before his audience. He writes very little down, spins off all his poems from memory and manages to make being meaningful look all too easy. Part of his talent is just that he is Franklin; the other part is hours of hard work to make what he does seem effortless. And then there is Randy Braithwaite, a young Jamaican exile. His poems chronicle the lives of everyone from Haile Selassie to Edward Seaga, and, as he says, the little people of the island that history forgot. At one time or another I have read on programs with all of them, and it was Franklin's idea that we form a group. I think what appealed to all of us most was that the concept of Poets Inc. thrives on our distinctiveness as poets and does not require that we become homogenized.

October 3:

Read tonight at a women's bookstore in Queens. The women gathered were enthusiastic and passionate in their attention, in other words, the perfect audience. I read "The Netherlands" publicly for the very first time. I thought this was the perfect audience to read the poem to. It is a poem that I cannot read just *anywhere.*

November 18:

Syrian has been nominated for an American Academy Award. At her last-Friday-in-the-month soiree last night, in her apartment, surrounded by a cadre of younger poets, Syrian doubted that she would win and said that her nomination was a brave show of tokenism. I have attended Syrian's salons sporadically. Each month she "presents" a poet to everyone gathered. The group consists of her fans, hangers-on, friends, lovers past and present, students past and present, and an inexhaustible supply of poets wanting desperately to be published.

Dec. 2:

Laura Castillo is a Mexican painter and the girlfriend of one of Neil's buddies. We went to the opening of an exhibition of her work at a gallery in the Village last night. The small space was filled with huge canvases of her in flight, her long red hair flowing as she floated over New York City and a host of other settings. There were nude sketches of herself and a plethora of other varied self-portraits. I admired her guts more than her paintings, which were competent and only mildly interesting. The imagination that allows her to envision herself in flight, to make herself her favorite subject, amazed me and I cheered. Neil called her inspiration narcissism pure and simple. But that is an instinct generally so underdeveloped in women that I forgave the lack of humility in her work and toyed with the idea that one day I might try to fly too.

self portrait

(for a woman painter i know)

the canvas rejoices
in the extraordinary nature
of yourself
unearthed
restored
recognized as a masterpiece

only once
is it impossible
to
pick up the brush
take the first step

mix the colors
that reveal
who you want to be

when it is done
the world knows
you are here

Jan. 4:

I now have enough rejection slips from the major poetry magazines to paper the bathroom walls. Two years' worth of submissions and two publications is all I have to show. When I told Syrian this she said it took her five years to get her first poem published in a "major" poetry magazine. But she says I am good enough and she says it is time. Although she has now become a part of the "poetry establishment" in a sense because of who publishes her books, and the access she now has to different kinds of audiences, institutions, grants, etc., Northstar Press, she insists, will always exist as an alternative press. Her decision to publish my manuscript *Full Circle* is far from momentous, but this decision has altered permanently my small cosmos.

January 20:

The high school students I am teaching creative writing to as resident artist, for the semester at PS 150, have challenged me to prove the relevance of poetry to their lives. We've read lots of Langston Hughes and they beg for more of his work. I am trying to convince them that poetry is not separate from everything else, but rather that it flows from it. So I have them write about arguments with parents, disappointing love affairs, hateful teachers, passing a test, even the desire for designer jeans, and how those experiences make them feel.

The biggest obstacle to their self-expression is not technical but rather that very few people have asked them what they think. Their teachers request the correct answer, not their opinion. Their parents, obedience, not what they want. So they come to me defensive, sometimes impenetrable. And yet what they do finally release/unleash in their poetry convinces me that their cynicism is justified. The only thing I can offer them in class is an antidote called art.

Aisha

RASHEED told me when he's out not to let any men in the house. Not a repairman, not a visitor. Not even somebody he knows. And nowadays when I go out, and take the twins, when we get back, he leads them into their bedroom and asks if I talked to any men on the street or if any men tried to talk to me. They stand before him scared and confused, resisting the nickels and quarters he holds before their eyes. They look at Rasheed and then at me. And what they learn about us in these moments turns them moody and irritable.

"You tell me anything you see, anything you know's not right," he warns them, looking at his children as if he trusts them as little as he now trusts me. And standing before him, the fear in their eyes makes me wonder who Rasheed has become. "You hear what I say?" he asks, pressing the money into their hands, forcing their palms open and then closing them tight. I watch my children promise to obey, and see them turn around, surprised to see me looking at them. Then they run past me into the living room and let the coins fall from their hands onto the dining room table. Quiet and amazed, they watch the money spin on its side and then noisily collapse. They stare at the coins a long time, almost

152

like they're waiting for them to start spinning again on their own. And finally they look at me and dash out the front door like children running away from home.

I don't know what I did. That's the part that hurts the most. He'd gotten almost halfway on the new house. Was working like a demon to finish it. Had even hired a couple of men to help him on it. Then all of a sudden he started slowing down, wasn't working as hard on it as he did before. And all the time he used to spend working on the house, he started spending watching me. He started staying home all the time. Turned over the running of the stores to Randy. And the only reason I could see that he was staying home was to see what I was doing. If I'd leave one room to go to another, I could feel his eyes on me like a weight.

And then, seemed like I didn't do anything right. He started complaining about the meals, how I ironed the clothes, even how I disciplined the children. One day I came into his study and found him sitting there with tears in his eyes. I asked him what was wrong. He just shook his head and waved me out of the room. Then after his last birthday, after he turned fifty-four, that's when he changed with me. Couldn't stand me to be out of his sight, but when we were together he wouldn't say a word.

When he first started doing this, I didn't know what to do. And at night when he'd want me I'd pull away. The kids would wake up in the morning and find me sleeping on the sofa. But then Rasheed saw my anger as proof I had something to hide. So now I talk to him even though I'm not saying anything I really feel. And I let him have me at night, not because I want to, but because it's my duty.

I don't know what inspires him. But Rasheed didn't change by himself. I changed too. Muhammad is almost a year and a half now. And we decided he would be our last child. I'm so used to being with the children that when I'm around adults I hardly know what to say. And the children grow so fast that soon they won't even need me. I help Tariq and Tameka with their homework at night, watch them count on their fingers, listen to them read storybooks to me. I've seen every moment of their lives and yet I didn't see them grow with so much determination. They'll always be my children but every day they belong, more than they did the day before, to themselves.

And I'm filled with a longing for a thing I can't name but that I feel. I asked Rasheed if I could take a course that Sister Khadija told me about. She and some other people in the mosque are taking a class over at N.Y.U. on the Middle East, Religion and Politics, taught by a famous Islamic scholar and writer. I even thought it was a class Rasheed and me could take together. Mama said she'd watch the kids on the nights we had the class. But Rasheed said I couldn't take it. "None of those things outside our home matters." That's what he told me. "Your life is here, in this house. With me and our children. Everything else is designed to tempt you away from me."

Sounded like he was pronouncing some kind of sentence on me with those words, and I started whimpering. I fell on my knees and asked him again. I was begging him over and over and he still said no. He just let me kneel on the floor before him, grabbing at his pants legs, pulling on him like Malika still sometimes pulls on me. And on the floor, with him watching me, I didn't know how I'd ever get up off my knees and call myself his wife again. I wanted to stay on the floor, to roll myself up in a ball and shut my eyes and not exist. But I couldn't stop the tears. And I soon knew that I was crying for more than him not letting me take that course. I was mourning what I was scared I'd never be.

He just stood and watched me and finally pulled me by the shoulders up on my feet.

"Don't ever do that again. Not for anything," he said. "Not to me or anybody else. You don't understand, you never really have, what you mean to me. What our marriage is about. I gambled on you and won. My brother said, 'I'll give you and that young girl a year.' My sister called me a fool. And when you started having babies they asked me what I was trying to prove. I never said a word to you about it. But for a long time, I counted the days, each one we were together. Then you had Muhammad and I could tell from everything about you that you were a woman and that you would stay. And I'm not gonna give you a chance to leave me now." "Where would I go," I screamed at him. Felt like my body was turning to jelly I was wanting so bad to sink back down on the floor, feeling that was where I really belonged. But he didn't say anything, just turned his back on me.

"And I'm lonely," I whined.

"Lonely? With four kids and a husband? Who else do you want? What more do you want?" He had whirled around and looked at me with so much anger I felt like I was going to melt. And so I told him, "Nothing, there's nothing more I want. Nothing more I need."

"I know what it is. It's your friends, those letters from Serena, the visits from Crystal. You're looking at their lives and wishing you were them."

"No, Rasheed, that's where you're wrong. I only want to be me."

Rasheed

EVERY week I come in and find a different house. She's gone through it during the day when I'm out and unleashed some kind of madness. And so the house keeps getting changed over and over again. She's always busy with some project. Once she took on the attic, sanded its floors, polished them so slick they were like an ice skating rink, papered the walls, put up curtains she made, placed throw rugs on the floor and decorated the area with secondhand furniture. She said we could use it as a guest room. But except for Carrie and a few people from the mosque, we never have company and especially not anybody who'd stay overnight. Then one time she moved the twins into the room Malika and Muhammad share and then changed her mind and moved them all back again. The furniture in the living room is rearranged so often the twins and me invented a game. As we come in the house after I pick them up from school, we try to guess where the sofa will be and where she's put the coffee table. The kitchen was once painted twice in six months. She fills the house with plants and just as the house gets moist and warm with their smell, stacks them on the back porch, putting odd miniature figurines in their place.

A WOMAN'S PLACE

I come home and find her splattered with paint or standing in the middle of the basement in a pile of plaster or maybe sitting at the sewing machine like somebody possessed, making another pair of curtains we don't need. It hurts my heart to see her this way. The heart she thinks I don't have. There are times when I can't look at her. I can't look at what I've done. She thinks I don't understand. But she's doing to this house what I won't let her do to us.

It was when I started building the new house. That's when I started feeling old. Got short of breath fast. Couldn't take too much sun and I don't have the energy I used to. But I didn't want Aisha to know it. So I started acting forceful and strong here in the house where it was easy, and I didn't need physical strength but just a strong will. Then I started having these dreams about her leaving me. Dreams where I was sick in bed, hooked up to a machine, and when I opened my eyes I saw Aisha's face and heard her telling me good-bye. She'd been trying to get me to the doctor's for a checkup for years, and after those dreams started I finally went. He told me I had hypertension. Put me on a special diet and gave me a bunch of pills. That's when I knew I was old. And that's when I turned against her, I think for no other reason than that she's young.

Aisha

WEEKDAY mornings I stand at the kitchen window and watch my street empty of cars. They pull out of driveways, roar away from the fronts of houses like mine, with an air of anticipation. Rasheed drives the twins to a Muslim school in Brooklyn, and from the backseat of the car they wave good-bye to me. Watching my neighbors, my husband and children leave the block each morning, filled with a sense of purpose, I wonder what I'll do the rest of the day. Sometimes I take Malika and Muhammad over to mama's and spend the afternoon in Manhattan. It's like a foreign country to me now. The city's pace makes me feel alive. But it exhausts me, too, and I nearly always fall asleep in the car going home when Rasheed picks us up.

Today Crystal is coming to visit. I feel Muhammad tugging at the hem of my robe and turn around to see Malika stuffing gobs of soft butter into her mouth at the kitchen table. I pick up Muhammad and grab a cloth from a chair and wrap him on my back. I wipe Malika's hands and face and lead her into the sewing room. Rasheed bought me a loom, and on it, I weave wall hangings. I've taped brown paper to the walls of the room and Malika and Muhammad's scribbles and colorful water paintings give the room a playful air. Word has gotten around the neighborhood and some of the women on the street buy my wall hangings. I even make them to order. But I usually sell them for much less than they're worth. It's hard for me to know how to judge their value. I weave to keep my mind busy, nothing more. I've done wall hangings for children's rooms with zebras and giraffes, clouds and moons with smiling faces, and a series of wall hangings of Africa based on descriptions in Serena's letters. I'm so good now, it's like my fingers do all the thinking for me. Malika and Muhammad are playing with a pile of yarn in one corner; the October sun warms the room. And I hear myself humming. . . . I almost remember how it feels to be happy.

When Crystal came in the afternoon, I showed her the letter from Serena that came a few days ago.

"Do you think she's ever coming back?" I asked when Crystal had read the letter.

"She'll come back. And she'll be the same. I can tell from what she writes."

Crystal stretched out on the sofa and watched me fold the letter and put it back in my dress pocket. We had spent the afternoon talking, and now Crystal lay watching me cutting the ragged edges off a wall hanging. Her eyes, however, kept returning to a stack of books I'd shown her. Thick heavy texts on history and religion and literature that I'd checked out of the library.

"So what do these books do for you?" she asked, picking up an anthology of modern poetry.

"They take me outside this house," I said, running into the kitchen to pull Muhammad out of the refrigerator where he was rummaging through the vegetable bin.

"And what do you do there?"

"Try to put things together the way I didn't know how to do before. I try to figure out what the Civil War has to do with me sitting on Riverdale Drive, in my house waiting for my husband to come home."

"Is there a connection?"

"You know there is as well as I do." I laughed as I placed Muhammad in his high chair. "When I was at Winthrop, I always felt that I wasn't good enough for the type of education they were offering me. They made me feel like I had to earn the right to be there. One day I'm going back to school and get some education that has to be good enough for me."

"What does Rasheed think about all this?"

"He doesn't know. I hide the books from him. Under the bed or in the children's room."

"Why?"

"He told me once that he hadn't read very much but that almost every book he read changed him. If he sees those books he'll think I'm trying to do the same."

"When do you read?"

"When he's not here."

"And when he is here?"

"I feel sometimes like he's not. I feel like I'm alone."

"What's gone wrong?"

"I don't know."

"Will you stay with him?"

"It's not so easy for me to consider leaving. Not like maybe it would be for you, Crystal. This is my house. These are my children. This is my family. What you see is everything I always wanted when I was growing up. And it's still everything I want now." I sat down and spread peanut butter and jelly on a slice of bread for Malika. "Sometimes Allah gives you what you want, and gives it to you with a vengeance, just to see if you're big enough to handle it."

"Or if you can survive it," Crystal said.

"I'll survive it," I told her. "I'm a mother. I have to; the world depends on me."

"I wrote a poem yesterday asking how one survives being in love," she said, lighting a cigarette. "Neil wants me to marry him and I don't know what to say. Foolishly, I thought being in love would be enough, be its own reward. But how can I marry a man my father refuses to meet? How can I *not* marry a man who has cared for me in the manner Neil has? How can I consider complicating my life this way? Yet I don't want to even think about how complicated my life would be without him."

Crystal looked at her watch and said, "I'd better be going, it's almost three o'clock. Rasheed will be home with the kids soon."

Some afternoons Rasheed has come in and found us in the living room or kitchen talking, and his eyes have roamed over Crystal's uncovered head, the curves revealed by her sweater and the tailored slacks she likes to wear, and his eyes spit out everything he sees. He's always telling me, "She's like a lot of those overeducated women. Nobody can tell her anything." I think it's Crystal's style, the way she talks and carries herself, that makes Rasheed feel like he just came up here from Georgia. He's always telling me not to try to be like her. Days when he's found her here he starts complaining about the house the minute he comes in. A saucer in the sink means I haven't done a thing all day. If the children's room is messy that means I don't care about them.

But what finished Crystal for Rasheed was the day he came home early to find us in my sewing room, Crystal giving me a massage. I'd been complaining about how tight I felt in my shoulders and back. So Crystal had me lie on a mat on the floor and gave me a rubdown. Soon as we heard the front door close, I got up. My heart was pounding like I'd done something wrong. Rasheed got to the doorway of the room just in time to see me stepping into my skirt and Crystal wiping mineral oil from her hands. I didn't have my blouse on and my head was uncovered. I couldn't think, couldn't move. And I could even tell that Crystal, standing next to me, was scared. He grabbed me and slapped me across the face, then threw me against the wall. The only sound I heard was my back making the brown paper with the children's pictures crumple as a sliver of blood flowed from my bottom lip.

"And you," he said to Crystal, "get out of here. If I ever catch you playing games again with my wife I can promise you a taste of the same."

"Rasheed, please don't," I cried.

"Shut up."

Crystal walked past him into the living room, and I heard her gathering her things. Then Rasheed asked me, "Did Malika and Muhammad see you two together?"

"What do you mean?"

"Did they see her touch you?"

I knew what he meant and I just lost, all of a sudden, some respect, some feeling for him I'd been holding on to because if I let it go I didn't know if I could live with him.

That was months ago, and I kept begging Crystal to come to see me anyway. I could visit her, Rasheed wouldn't have to know or find out. But it wouldn't be the same. When she comes to see me, she brings more than herself. She brings something of the world I gave up to be Rasheed's wife. And she brings Winthrop and Serena and everything I thought one day I might have. She brings a way for me to keep on going. Different as we are, Crystal brings me myself, every time she steps through that door.

I stood watching her put on her jacket and heard her tell me, "I'm not coming again. I shouldn't have. You'll just have to come to Manhattan."

"You're right. It's just that as long as you still came to see me, I could convince myself this was my life I was living and not his, after all."

Crystal

THE restaurant was too expensive. The china and glassware, finely wrought sculptures designed more for aesthetics than function. The single red rose craning its leafed neck out of the silver vase in the center of the table seemed to promise that the aura of the room—pale blue and white, with circular tables draped in starched ruffled cloths, drenched in the perfume of overconfidence—and the food, supposedly among the best served in the city, would satisfy needs more subtle and complex than mere nourishment of the body. I sipped an aperitif from an elegant glass that, as I assessed it closely, filled my mind with lines from Shakespeare and colors from Romare Bearden. What, I wondered, was my brother trying to prove by asking me to meet him here.

Obviously that he could afford it, or that his firm could. In town on business for the Chicago law firm of which he is an associate, he called the night before and suggested we have lunch.

When I saw him at the entrance, the first thing I noticed was a cranberry colored handkerchief, playful and rakish, poking out of his breast pocket. He had put on weight since I saw him last, but as he walked toward me behind the waiter, I made a mental note not to mention this. His dark blue suit and pale gray shirt matched the decor of the room. Casually looking around, Brad appeared to both hope and fear that someone he knew might see him. His face, graced by a mustache, exuded a confidence that was almost contagious. He kissed me patronizingly, then sat down. I had forgotten how smoothly handsome my brother really is. We ordered drinks, and he studied my face dramatically with just a touch of the clown.

"You look good," he said.

"You sound surprised."

"Maybe I am."

"Have you talked to father lately?" I asked, passing over the pain inflicted by his remark.

"About two weeks ago. Did he tell you he's decided to retire?"

"No, no, he didn't tell me all that," I conceded. Only my father and I know, really, how estranged we are, how little is said that matters or that changes things during the conversations that result from my regular calls home once a month. Calls I must find the courage to make. And I think I could withstand total rejection easier than the disinterest that greets me, the words that feign nonchalance but that ring with disapproval nonetheless. He is waiting for me to say I am sorry. I am waiting to hear him say I love you anyway.

The waiter brought our salads, and as I poured vinegar and oil over mine, Brad asked, "By the way, how's your white boy?"

"Look, let's not talk about Neil. We don't have to and I'd prefer if we didn't."

"Why so touchy?"

"Touchy? Why so rude, why so insensitive, I should ask you."

"Look, I just asked."

"You didn't ask anything. You threw down a gauntlet. You drew a sword, like you always do."

164

"Okay. Okay." He backed off. I recalled the one time Neil and Brad had met, at my insistence, over drinks. Brad had turned before my eyes into the laid-back, belligerent, super-cool eighteen-year-old he had been the summer after high school. He spent that summer smoking joints and hanging out at the neighborhood playground with a group of young toughs who viewed his entry into their world as a victory. And two weeks before he was due to leave for college, he left the group and never went back. But that evening with Neil he adopted the same sullen air that had marked him that summer. Neil jabbered on, embarrassed and ridiculous in the face of Brad's brooding, his refusal to look him in the eye and his insistence on reaching for my hand throughout the evening as though we were lovers instead of siblings. In the taxi home, Neil had fumed, "Now we're even. My father. Your brother." The next day Brad called and asked me in the hushed tones of an obscene caller, "Why a white boy? Just tell me that."

My father's preparation of his only son for success was rigorous and faithful. Every choice my brother ever made has been calculated. At ten he made up a list of what he wanted to be when he grew up. At twelve father began taking him to the library to help him do research on each career. At fourteen they started choosing colleges. At fifteen he picked the three colleges he would apply to and at seventeen he underwent interviews at each one. One Christmas when I was home from Winthrop and Brad was still in high school, I overheard Brad and my father talking about graduate schools. In exasperation I asked father why he didn't allow Brad to leave one acre of his existence to chance, why they were drawing his life as intently as a map. My father said scornfully, "Our women just can't stand to see this much confidence in their men. Go on in the other room with your mother if it's too much for you to witness."

And soon Brad went to Dartmouth and then to Harvard Law and married the daughter of a proper black Brahmin family from Boston. He has chosen everything in his life, from his neighborhood to his car, with the same staunch determination. He and father are very proud of him. Mother is too. But I tremble. And he has asked me why I *chose* Neil, why I *decided* to love a white man. Yet the unintentional, improbable nature of what happened in my heart and Neil's would bore my brother even if he understood it.

So I sat across from him and announced, "He's asked me to marry him."

Brad put down his fork and asked incredulously, "Are you going to do it?"

Although I had not made a decision, I heard myself saying, "Yes, I am."

"Hell, it's your life. But tell me this—why do you want to make it more difficult than it has to be? Aren't there enough hurdles, enough risks, just to be black, a woman, a poet? For Christ's sake, think about what you're doing."

"Why are you so afraid of my life? The trinity you just described like a crucifix is all I've got. And I won't let you or anybody smash it."

"What black person will believe anything you write now?"

"If credibility is lost so easily, maybe it's not worth it."

"Crystal, I want you to be happy."

"You only want what's best for *you*. Me, living a life that leaves all your prejudices undisturbed. You and father think it's Neil you hate. You really hate me. If you didn't you could leave me alone. You could understand me like before and know that I still know who I am."

"Do you? Do you still know who you are?" he asked with quiet bitterness. "I don't think so."

"Until now, I thought I knew who you were," I shouted. "Maybe I don't know that either." I pulled on my coat and left the table. The rest of the afternoon I paced Fifth Avenue, pushing through the crowds, gazing absently into store windows. Finally I went into a gleaming hulk of chrome and glass—a fifty-six-story tower that contained an atrium space. I drank half a bottle of Chablis and watched a pianist in tie and tails play Cole Porter tunes on a baby grand in the center of the cavernous entranceway. And by the time I walked back onto Fifth Avenue I had decided to marry Neil.

Our wedding was not a celebration but rather an omen. My father and brother did not come. Serena sent a telegram saying that a coup attempt had resulted in the closing of the airport in Nairobi and the imposition of a state of emergency. Since Carla had divorced him, Neil's father could not stand to be in the same room with her so he sent us a check for five hundred dollars. The handwriting on the check and the card was so haphazard Neil barely recognized it and said it made him think of the careening sound of his father's voice when they spoke by phone every few months.

A sunny, luminous morning broke into a heavy downpour as we entered City Hall trailed by Aisha, Carla, mother and two of Neil's friends. Those absent chiseled the rhythm of their private and political battles onto the surface of that day. And I required, much more than I knew then the presence of everyone who wasn't there. The absences, whether legitimate or carved from the stone of bitterness and jealousy, slit the skin of my confidence. And the reception in our apartment, where Aisha had to leave early because Rasheed had not really wanted her to come, and Carla cornered me and thrust upon me the details of her love affair with a feminist lawyer in San Diego, and Neil's friends drank too much, all confirmed every doubt I had yet to overcome.

We flew to San Juan and spent a week there. I lay on the beach beside Neil waiting to feel like a different person. I did not. I waited for this new feeling to capture me because I knew we had moved to a more perilous level of love. I knew that if we were blessed nothing would change and yet everything would be different. But I still did not know if I had married Neil despite my father's warning or because of it.

Neil

I WAS the one who wanted to get married. I knew she was unsure, still wanting to wait until her old man came around. Having things in their place, neatness and order, mean a lot to her, whether it's her desk or her life. And she's one of the few people I know who thinks the same principles that apply to a desk can be applied to life. Her mother came up a few months ago to visit us. And this visit, which I had thought would vindicate the past two years, had more the feel of a refutation of Crystal's father about it than an acknowledgment of us. Marriage, I thought, would give Crystal a way to tell the world to go to hell. But I'm less sure of her now than before. What would her father's approval mean to her, if suddenly, magically, by renouncing me, she gained it back? We've talked about this and she's admitted that she longs not so much for the time before she met me, but the time before she became a woman to be judged rather than a child to be loved.

A few weeks before the wedding her second book was published and her friend and publisher, Syrian, gave a small party for her. Syrian's apartment was filled with writers, musicians, literary types, and I was the only white person there. I still can't get over how much this bothered me.

Maybe I'm not as liberal as I thought. I know now that I'm not as secure.

Everybody was polite. But there was a lot going on that had to do with me that I couldn't hear or see but that I could feel. I could feel it in how people looked at Crystal differently when Syrian introduced me as Crystal's fiancé, I could feel it in the way some people talked to me with a condescending, irritating patience reserved for idiots and white people they feel superior to. It was Crystal's night and I was proud of her. She was surrounded by people most of the time. Yet when we got home I picked a fight, complained she'd ignored me the whole evening. It ended with her angry and not speaking and me sitting in the living room in front of the television till 3 A.M.; that's how long it took me to get up the nerve to go back into the bedroom. And now we're married. She's my wife. But I still don't feel that she is really mine.

Crystal

I THOUGHT I had more courage. But I don't know how to rise to the occasion of a life with him. With my husband, I am a stranger and a sojourner. I thought no one else mattered. But I am the world, its censure, its all too faint wisdom, its confusion, meanness, doubt. And like the world, I am capable of any act to save myself from what I do not understand.

With him, I felt certain I could pay any price for what I feel. Yet my imagination was neither reckless nor bold enough to conceive of the price I am paying.

The man resembled a beached whale. His body, racked by a growling chorus of snores as he lay in the middle of the disheveled motel bed, was graceless, inspiring reflections that distracted me from him and the sexual conspiracy that had bound us only hours before. A beached black whale. The thought was metaphoric but ludicrous. Still, that is how I would've described him in a poem. As I watched the stranger to whom I had made love, instinctively I mined the meaning of our fleeting, unexpected alliance for something I could salvage and turn into restorative, telling beauty. Through a veil of smoke from my third cigarette, however, I heard no echoes of song. I could not have acknowledged a melody even if one were possible, and one was not. Last night I had wanted the man. But the desire was rooted in the earth of muddled illusions that have spawned a will that terrifies and amazes me. At four o'clock in the morning I woke up beside him burdened with a victory I no longer wanted. Stripped of glasses, his face was devoid of the allure that had hovered and enticed at last night's reception. His hands, cupped at his groin, were tranquil. At midnight they had tamed me like an eighth continent.

My fingers trembled and I dropped the cigarette, its bright red tip burning a tiny ashen hole in the green carpet. I bent to pick it up, and as I sat back in the chair, looked through the half-parted curtains at the sunrise. Since this stranger did not inspire, I vowed to write instead about that sky, and morning exploding in a war dance of color that cleansed and forgave. But at the thought of forgiveness, I felt my nakedness as an indictment. I stood, put on my kimono, sighing at the feel of silk dripping over my shoulders. Tying the belt around my waist tightly, I heard the man's snores stall as though swallowed in a ravenous gulp.

Since I scrambled out of bed and took refuge in the room's only chair an hour and a half ago, my glance had been repeatedly drawn to him by some anxious, insatiable curiosity. The kind that produces crowds jostling for a clear view at the scene of a disaster. As I looked at him one last time, I wondered if, when I returned home, I would continue to look at Neil with shuttered eyes longing for retreat. And what he would do if I did.

Last night's reading was arranged as part of a series of events celebrating the eighth anniversary of the Creative Writing Program at Winthrop, and as a way to promote my second book, *Unclaimed Heart*. I spent the entire day on campus, talking with young, fervently talented would-be poets, discussing my work, meeting faculty members in the program and reading from my two books in the evening.

I read my poetry and answered questions, some foolish,

most ordinary, a few so surprisingly brilliant I wanted to thank those who asked them. And while I was doing this, I struggled to accomplish in public what has eluded me in private—to bare my soul yet protect it from careless, lethal dissection.

I am in the throes of an infidelity at once premeditated and random. And all the lovers I have taken are black. I am burdened and imprisoned, for the etiquette of infidelity puzzles me. I don't know how to tell a man I don't want to wake up beside him. And so I am haunted by sins other women dismiss from their lives by merely opening the doors to their rooms.

After years of allegiance to the cerebral in my poetry, I have discovered the nobility of passion. And more successfully than I imagined possible, fused intellect with ardor. The poetry is almost easy. Now it is my life that I approach each day with the conviction that I simply cannot do it.

I sat on the stage in Hawthorne Hall watching the audience shift in anticipation. Listened as I was described as a talented alumna and a poet whose work was a reflection of the turmoil and promise of the times. I am the poem, not just the poet. Each time I give a reading, impatient, hungry eyes fondle me. Each verse is the wafer pressed to waiting tongue tip. And the audience's acceptance of my vision is evidence that I belong to them in a way I can never escape.

I gazed absently at the domelike ceiling overhead, and in my mind, switched off the voice of the student nervously plodding through the introduction. How little I remembered from all the classes and papers. The reading lists and weekends spent in Randall Library taught me virtually nothing of use in navigating my way through the dogged ordinariness of my days. The sound of applause stifled my reverie. Forcing a gracious smile I did not feel, I stood and walked to the lectern.

Kate Flanner introduced me to the man. She must be fifty-five by now, I thought as I saw her ruddy, rawboned

face moving toward me, pushing through the crowd. Kate
Flanner was the first person who told me I should write. I
signed up for every course she taught at Winthrop, followed
her back to her office after class to finish classroom discus-
sions and to watch her gray eyes begin to sparkle as she
talked with equal ease about Thackeray, Kafka or Jean
Toomer. She told me about studying at the Sorbonne, living
in Europe for nearly a decade. Over the years I've written to
her, and she has always answered, with one page, succinct,
treasured letters that gave me a sense of her life and her
continued faith in my talent. I looked up to her too much to
ever really be her friend. And yet just knowing that Kate is
somewhere out there has meant a lot to me. Still, none of
this stopped me from betraying her.

As she walked toward me I noticed that she had a black
man, literally in tow, following her.

"You were wonderful, just wonderful," she said, smiling
eagerly. "There's someone I want you to meet," she told
me, turning dramatically to the man standing behind her.
"This is Leonard St. Martin, he's an adjunct professor in the
English department. He writes too." Kate squeezed the
man's arm possessively.

"I try my hand at a short story now and then," he said
offhandedly in a faintly West Indian accent, his eyes meeting
Kate's as if for a cue.

"He's brilliant. He just doesn't want to admit it," Kate
said fondly. Her cheeks were flushed and she appeared
almost girlish. She flourished beside him like a spring
flower blooming brazenly in the unobstructed rays of the
sun.

"Have you been published?" I asked.

"Not yet."

"The English department has started a literary magazine
and I'm the editor. Leonard will have a piece in it when it
debuts in the spring," Kate assured us both. A voice summoned her from the other side of the hall and she excused
herself.

"Kate's a remarkable woman," the man said, watching her leave.

"She was one of the best teachers I had."

"What was it like when you were here?" he asked, turning back to me.

"I don't know if schools like Winthrop really change. It's probably a lot now like it was then."

"And how was it then?"

"Elitist. Exhilarating."

"It's a lot like that now." He laughed. And the laughter gave breadth to his face, which had seemed a flat, joyless plain.

"What do you teach?" I asked.

"The Afro-American novel. They offered me a full-time position but I turned it down."

"Why?"

"I'm afraid that if exploring a subject that fascinates me became a job instead of an avocation, it would destroy everything that keeps me interested in it. Anyway, how do you feel coming back?"

"Actually, I'm surprised by how little I've felt on seeing it all again. When I was here it was sometimes unbearable, and yet I didn't want to be anywhere else." As I reminisced, startled by the intimacy of my words, our eyes collided and our smiles wordlessly designed a code that was broken when we both grew silent, overwhelmed by our mutual discovery of desire.

"I live in Portland, Maine," he told me suddenly, defusing our gazes. "Where I'm trying to finish my doctoral thesis. Please don't ask me what it's on. The damn thing is waiting for me at home like a neglected wife. I don't want to ruin the evening thinking about it."

"All right," I promised, deciding, as I did, to sleep with him that night.

Before he drove me to the motel where I was staying, he left to tell Kate where he was going. Kate followed him back to me.

"What time will you be leaving for New York?" she asked.

"My flight's at nine o'clock."

"I'm so proud of you. We all are," Kate assured me earnestly. Then she turned to Leonard and gazed at him as though fearing she might never see him again.

"I'll call you in the morning," he told her, pulling on his gloves and trading some secret reassurance with her through his glance.

"Do you love her?" I asked him in the car.

"She's got cancer. For the past six months it's been in remission."

"She didn't tell me."

"Only a few people know. Anyway, her greatest need right now is to believe she'll never die. When she's with me, she feels that's a distinct possibility."

"Are you proud of that?"

"I never thought of it that way, but yes, I guess I am."

At the hotel, he escorted me to my room and, uninvited, followed me in. And just before he kissed me he asked, "Do you love your husband?" I told him that I did. And that, I knew more certainly than anything else, was the truth.

Neil

SHE told me she had a debt to pay. That's how she explained what she was doing. I watched Crystal putting clean sheets and a comforter on the sofa bed in her study and wondered what she had taken and from whom that demanded replacement. Smoothing the newly made bed with her hands, she sat down and looked at me like I was a stranger annoying her in a public place.

"I just need to be alone for a while. I can't sleep with you now, Neil. Not until it's finished."

"Until what's finished?"

"There's something I have to do. A debt I have to pay."

"Are you sick? Is that it?"

She erupted into laughter so brutal it drove me from the room. So that night I didn't bother her. I know her moods, and when her writing is going well, she always withdraws, into herself. I've learned to live with her penchant for solitude. And even when I found out about the other men I refused to believe she was punishing me because I'm white. It made no sense. But when I told her that, she said, "It makes all the sense in the world. But really, this has nothing at all to do with you."

"You're talking about our marriage and you say it's got nothing to do with me."

"I didn't mean it like that."

"You bitch," I shouted, rising from my chair. "You heartless arrogant bitch."

And as I moved toward her, she gazed at me as if relieved that what she had expected would finally happen. And as I gripped her shoulders, balled my hand into a fist and prepared to strike her, I remembered the numbing silence that settled over our house after my father had beaten my mother, and the night I watched him slamming her again and again against the walls, sat and watched when her screams woke me from a nap on the sofa. Sat paralyzed, rooted to the sofa, watched them, praying that I was still asleep and that what I was watching was a dream. Crystal's cowering, expectant face was all I could see, and it made me want to close my eyes forever.

I released her and walked instead to the bedroom, locked the door and lay on the bed in the dark. My hands still shook with the force of the unmet desire to hurt her. So I stretched my arms out at my sides and willed my hands to be as stiff and silent as corpses.

I've always liked the dark, felt somehow that it made you safe, that whatever you couldn't see couldn't touch you. The dark is where I'd hide when my parents fought. I'd run inside the closet and cover my ears with the hems of coats hanging there, so I couldn't hear their voices. It was dark, and even when my old man yanked the closet door open and pulled out his jacket, ready to storm out of the house, I wasn't noticed or discovered. My father slammed the closet door, extinguishing the intruding light. But he was never able to block out the sound of my mother breaking dishes in the kitchen, throwing them onto the floor, smashing glasses against the walls, and my sister, five years older than me and who hated the dark, yelling for her to stop.

Sometimes I'd fall asleep. The dark, then, felt like my mother's lips on my forehead the times she remembered to kiss me good night. Like my father's hands steadying me on the seat, the summer he taught me to ride a two-wheeler. But I'd wake up suddenly when my sister opened the door. She loomed like a phantom, ordering me to come out, pulling me by the shoulders with both hands when I refused.

The dark helped me to survive my childhood but it failed to dissolve the wretchedness that washed over me in waves every time I thought of Crystal. The hatred I felt for her didn't vindicate me. For even as I tried to wallow in it, envisioned submitting her to terrible acts of cruelty and debasement I knew I could never commit, I realized that I still wanted her.

"This has nothing to do with you," she said. "Nothing to do with you." I'd been totally unaware of her talent for lies. And I hate her most because now I can never look at her again without seeing what she's done.

Serena

THE women are picking cotton. Standing at the
entrance to the village, I watch them in the field that
stretches against the horizon. They work, their backs bowed
beneath clouds that seem as fragile as the cotton balls filling
their palms. A group of baobab trees, their trunks sunk into
the reddish brown earth, limbs twisting in the shape of a
half-risen sun, squat at the edge of the field. The Shona
believe that even as the trees stand, timeless and elegant,
they shelter spirits ready to overtake any life within reach.
I've never seen a country more confident of its beauty. For
this sky and these trees alone the whites must have wanted
to stay. Every time I look closely at the land I know why they
fought so long and so hard never to give it back to whom
God gave it first. They swore, defiantly, "Never, in a thousand years." It took eighteen and now the women of this
village are harvesting their own cotton, sown on plots the
new black government has given them. Land sold by a
farmer whose great grandfather fled an overcrowded Liver-
pool for the vastness of this place. And the farmer himself
moved to Australia a month after the former guerrillas were
elected to rule the country.

The soil is lush, productive, almost as if the years of war, the blood and bones of black and white, have enriched it. Just last month I read a report from the ministry of agriculture predicting a bumper crop of maize, wheat and cotton.

The thick wool caps that some of the women wear, red, yellow, green, dot the field with color. They undulate across the land, their bags swelling with cotton as they progress. Yet even from this distance I can see the holes and tears in their skirts and blouses. Their fat arms and broad backs, toughened by the sun, shine like polished leather. Their hair, close cropped as a man's, exposes high-cheekboned faces. How have they endured? The labor is hard, repetitive, and asks them to be as strong as mules, as uncomplaining as sheep. What is marriage, what is love faced with the long absences of husbands and men, who before majority rule worked in cities most of the women never saw, or in the diamond mines the women witnessed in nightmares. How did they honor the men's return, once a year, once every two years, to plant the seed of life in them in a cycle as faithful as that which saw the women planting maize and shucking it months later. What do they feel when receiving the once-a-month letters stuffed with a meager but welcome portion of a meager pay? How have they worked season after season land that by custom and law only men can inherit? I look again at the sky—still, yet studded with brilliant blinding sunlight—but finding no answer there, I turn and head back into the village.

Today is my first full day in this, the last village on a tour of the rural areas for the Ministry of Women's Development. My driver, bodyguard and I arrived after dark last night, welcomed and offered a meal and a place to sleep by the chief. The circular thatched-roofed huts of the village were quiet then. As Samuel parked the Land-Rover, I saw only a few children running after-dinner errands, small shadowy figures, melding phantomlike into the silence of the evening. Today is the first day I've really seen the women. But I've seen them in all the other villages and townships we've been through. I've seen the same women eking out the same type of parched, sun-dried existence. I've seen the same neglect, the same illiteracy and ignorance, for which they pay with their lives. The government says there will be change. Tells these women it will come before they die. But if it comes, it'll come for their children —children like the ones we saw a few days ago along the highway as we were entering another township. There were as many, I guess, as fifty of them sitting beneath a baobab tree watching a teacher write a math exercise on a chalkboard propped up by a chair.

It was midday and the sun was unbearable. Yet the children's sweat-drenched faces followed each move of the chalk across the blackboard. And I'll always remember the sight of slender brown arms thrust into the air, fingers squirming in excitement as the teacher pointed to a boy who rose, shirtless, barefoot, in shorts tied at the waist by string, to give an answer that earned him applause from the children around him. Maybe the change will come in time for them. Maybe the promise, this time, won't be broken.

I've seen the same women and children in other villages but I know that these women and children are different. And as the women troop back into the village for lunch and rest, I see the evidence of war on their bodies. I see the woman who wears an eye patch, the young girl who hobbles on a maimed foot. These people spent a good part of the war in a guerrilla-controlled resettlement camp on the border with Zambia. Several months before the end of the fighting, the camp was raided by government soldiers. That day in the capital, the guerrilla leaders, representatives of the British and the Americans, and officials of the minority government met in a wood-paneled hall in Parliament House to continue their months-long efforts to negotiate peace. And at that moment fifteen hundred miles away, white soldiers who had painted their hands and faces black attacked the camp, killing most of the soldiers protecting it, in a surprise burst of fire from M-16s. The civilians were rounded up from tending small gardens, from cooking and from rest.

When the women saw the guns aimed at them, I imagine that some must've dropped to their knees in prayer. The babies on their backs, smelling the fear inside the beads of sweat on their mothers' necks and inhaling it, began crying as when first expelled from the womb. The soldiers pursued those who ran, smashing dead bodies with armored cars. Rifle butts knocked the women unconscious, knives slit their breasts, slashed their throats, and of the men there—mostly old and feeble—they cut off penises, arms and legs. Babies were smashed against the hoods of jeeps bought from the U.S. by South Africa and sent as an act of friendship to the minority government. And many of the women wondered, as soldiers grabbed them and prepared to kill them, wondered in the seconds they had left, gazing at the skin around the eyes that was not blackened, and at the thin lips twitching with hate, wondered why the gods of the whites had abandoned them. Why they had nothing more than death to believe in and fear. Three hundred people were killed that morning. When it was over, only the endless cries of a few toddlers crawling among the corpses, their fingers digging into the dusty dry earth, filled the air.

Those who escaped hid in the bush, where some died of their wounds. Those who survived ate worms and lizards, drank their own urine.

The camp sat odorous and defeated for three days before the guerrillas returned from their own raid and helped the survivors bury the dead. After the independence agreement was signed, the people who survived the massacre left the camp and began planting cotton on the former estate of Jonathan Leeds, now quite prosperously resettled in Sydney, Australia.

Nearly forty women sit before me, their bare calloused feet covered with dust. A few wear sneakers without laces or shower thongs worn down to the edge on one side. The toddlers and babies held in their arms wriggle restlessly, struggling for freedom. The older children, having finished a lunch of mealie-mealie scooped out of tin bowls with fingers or thick hunks of bread, chase one another raucously in the distance, wrestling and dancing in circles, their laughter and taunts a kind of music.

Samuel, the driver, sits outside the hut he and Renson, my bodyguard, shared, a transistor radio held tightly to his ear. And even in his khaki uniform he still manages to look like a hipster. It must be the sunglasses, I think, imagining his eyes closed tight behind them as his head bobs in time with the sound of Bob Marley's "Crazy Baldhead," drifting in spurts over to where the women and I sit.

The chief of the village walks toward us, his generous paunch appearing to precede him on its own. He's tall, a broadly built man without the hungry, tattered look of his people. In fact, he resembles nothing so much as a civil servant, dressed in a short-sleeved white shirt and trousers. Before the war there were over one thousand people in this village. There are five hundred now, almost three quarters of them women. As the chief nears us, the women shift in anticipation, shush older children, offer squalling babies a breast to suck, try vainly once more to smooth the wrinkles in their clothes and rivet their eyes on the chief. Wiping his face with a cloth and stuffing it into his pants pocket, the chief first greets the women as a group. They respond in a humble, reverent chorus. He tells them the purpose of my visit and commands them to listen to me. When he has finished, I don't tell the women that the ministry has sent me to evaluate and assess their status. And based upon what I've seen, to write a report that will be given to the prime minister to hopefully strengthen his commitment beyond rhetoric to women's rights. I tell them simply that I have come not to talk, but to listen.

So unused are they to telling others what they want that they sit before me in response to my request, whispering among themselves and eyeing me like one of their sex who might just possibly be mad.

Finally near the front a young woman stands up. "We need water nearby," she says timidly, stopping to look at the chief and at the other women for approval to continue. "We still trek for many miles bringing water from the streams." Her voice, which had trembled in an unsure whisper at first, steadies itself. The hands she had hidden behind her back become eloquent punctuations to her words, traveling over the heads of the other women, all turning away from me to her. "We need electricity, like there is in the larger townships. Our children need a school so they do not have to read under the hot sun." The other women are now stirring, murmuring in agreement, sitting straighter and marshaling their own sense of denial. "It has been two years since we won back our land," the woman charged. "We have seen no changes. Where is the revolution? When will it come to us?"

Another woman, fat, bulging, her arms and legs broad as tree stumps, hoists herself up onto her feet. Small rivers of sweat slide down her dark fleshy face. She yanks a soiled scarf from her head and wipes her neck, pointing, as she does, to the young girl beside her on the ground, one of the girl's legs cut off at the knee, a pink and brown stump of dry dead skin and flesh. "My daughter has not seen a doctor in months. Her leg is swelling and our own treatments have not healed it," she charges. The girl, whom I saw hobbling around the village on crutches, let her head drop like a beaten animal beneath her mother's pitying glance. "Why is it only the soldiers and the 'comrades' are seen by doctors? She lost her leg carrying maize to soldiers hiding in the bush. My daughter was a soldier too. We in this place have wounds. Wounds that have not healed in all this time." The other women shake their heads, erupt into a chorus of aahhhs and uh-huhs that bear witness to the woman and her child. The woman lowers herself, landing heavily on the ground beside her daughter, whom she pulls with one of her strong arms closer, pressing the girl's head onto her shoulder.

"What of the roads?" someone shouts, eager and testy. "Promises were made. Promises must be kept." The words are ominous and plaintive and instantly overtaken, hoisted into the air as broad as a banner, as the women break into a clamorous outcry of complaint. The bruised, never enough, relentless nature of their lives seems to strike them all at once. Suddenly the chief stands, his jowls bunched in amazement. Too harshly, he silences them, warning them to retreat into a humility they will never wear comfortably again.

"What of a bride price?" I ask when they are quiet. "The ministry wants to abolish it." A wave of laughter travels among them. And from the rear there is a shout, "There are so few men we fear many of us will never again have the need for bride price. We fear our daughters will not know it either. But bride price must be paid or the ancestors will make babies die in the womb and the marriage cannot survive. The ancestors will inflict the penalty on generations that follow." The women in the ministry have made stamping out the bride price and the remnants of polygamy a top priority. But they meet their stiffest resistance from women such as these. Women who with their children bore the brunt of the war and were not counted officially among the dead. Women who after all the years of fighting now want tradition and peace, men again, children and bride price. "You are like all the government people who tell us what we should want and don't listen to what we need," the first woman who had spoken says in exasperation. "Bring the revolution to us. That is all we ask."

I decided to go to bed early tonight, for in the morning we will leave at 5 A.M. for the capital. And as I study my face in the small cracked mirror hanging from the wall by a nail, I undress. I do this more now—study my face. Ever since I turned thirty, I appraise what I see every time I look in the mirror. My skin is darker from years of exposure to the sun. My body is leaner. Fat has turned, without my noticing, into muscle. My breasts are still formidable, but I've finally decided to call my body home and live in it in peace. As I meditate on the history and future of myself as revealed by my reflection, a breeze flutters the skimpy curtains at the window, bringing into the room a cool, almost cold wind. I lower the window, put on a cotton nightgown and crawl into bed.

I've seen a dozen countries. In Egypt I taught sociology at the American University in Cairo for two years and then worked with a UNESCO project that introduced birth control methods into rural areas in Somalia. I've lived in Kenya and Senegal. I speak Swahili, Arabic, French and three ethnic languages. I was an outsider in all those other countries, am an outsider even here. But I understand why. The culture, the soil, the languages aren't in my veins, although I can acquire and appreciate them. I understand that, and the understanding helps me accept my status as observer and only partial intimate.

The longer I'm here, the less I know, really, what or who Africa is. It's insurmountable, that I know. And always, it seems, I can be locked out, consigned to irrelevance. My mastery of one language gives me few clues to the hundreds of others that bond the people around me. My solidarity with the women does nothing to change their ultimate definition of me as a foreigner and therefore a permanent guest. And when I behold their lives, I wonder, had I been born here instead of Detroit, would fate have plucked me from the fields and installed me in a mission school? Spared me marriage at fifteen? Circumcision at birth? Yet all this has rooted me here, even as I war with it. I stay because in every country I've been witness to a nation's birth. And the often clumsy, ill-conceived process gains my loyalty each time. Nothing is more exciting to see than a people becoming a nation.

There is still, and perhaps will always be, Alhaji Ibrahim. Maybe it is he, after all the other men, whom I really love, if only because I can never have him. Never has he denied me anything I asked. And yet we both cherish my reluctance to ask of him everything I could. At a new address his letters reach me before any one else's. And he's the one who gave me the money to buy the land I want. For the past two years, since a coup ousted the country's first elected government in over a decade, he's been living in an exile of sorts in London.

Before the coup, he was implicated but not indicted in a scandal involving contracts for foreign businesses, and he wrote to me, shortly after he decided not to return to Nigeria, saying, "Because I knew the president and many others in the government, and because of my wealth, I'm certain a cell at Kirikiri has been reserved for me."

Six months after he settled in London, found a house and transferred his business affairs, he sent me a ticket, and arranged for me to stay for a week at the London Hilton. Once or twice a year we have met this way, ever since I left Nigeria, back in '80.

When I saw him last month, I finally asked him about the gossip, the news stories seeming to implicate him in the crimes of others.

I have seen him in Western-style suits, pinstriped, perfectly tailored. And it's hard to accept him dressed like that. He never seems as comfortable as when he's in his traditional robes, for they imbue him with a regal aura. And in them he exudes the persona of a man unaccustomed to being challenged. He sat across from me at the dinner table looking elegant, his robes billowing and turned up for convenience' sake at his shoulders, and seemed sincerely disappointed that I had found it necessary to question his honesty.

"If I am corrupt, there isn't a single honest man in Nigeria," he said defensively. "Not one."

"But it's important for me to know if what the papers say you did is true."

"I am wealthy. Is that a crime? But I am not wealthy because I stole from my country."

"Then why not go back?"

"One day I will. But not now. My association with the former government was too intimate. When the army boys step down or are themselves overthrown, then I'll return, not before."

"And what of the former president? Where is he?"

"Still under arrest. Held in some stinking jail with common criminals."

"Was he your friend?"

"He still is."

"Is he corrupt?"

"He is weak. And he overlooked the corruption of others. I remember the night our party won the election. The American-style election we were so proud of because it made us as 'legitimate' as politicians in the West. We were being driven to his headquarters, where he would make his acceptance speech. He turned to me and said, 'Now I tremble for myself and for this country.' "

" 'Why?' I asked him.

" 'Because I do not know how to rule eighty million people.'

" 'You've been in politics over twenty years,' I reminded him.

" 'Politics doesn't necessarily prepare one for leadership,' he said.

" 'I don't know what else could,' I told him.

"He sighed and laid his head against the window and then fell asleep. He only woke up when we arrived, and when he made his speech, there were tears in his eyes. Everyone thought he was overcome by emotion. I knew he was paralyzed by fear."

The Alhaji was silent, brooding on the fate of his friend. I assessed his smooth, wrinkle-free face, open and yet closed, the mustache that was barren of a single gray hair, and the bearing that in the face of this setback appeared more confident than ever.

"And even now there is talk of another coup," he said. "I've heard the rumors. Each clique, civilian or military, rules the country like a private fiefdom, now and then throwing a slogan or 'plan' to the people to keep them distracted from the hunger in their bellies or the absence of money in their pockets. I admit now that my generation failed Nigeria, as my generation failed Africa. But were we more brutal than the Europeans who trained us to walk in their shadow? More blind? We listened to and believed every paternalistic theory they devised about economics and growth even as we preached socialism and self-reliance. And now we are beggars as we have never been in a history that is longer and richer than any white man can imagine."

This admission quieted him for an embarrassed moment, and when he roused himself he looked squarely at me and said, "All right, I will give you the money you want, to buy this land. But tell me, what will you do with it? Why do you want it?"

"I want to start a women's farming cooperative on it, make it a place where women can bring their produce and sell it. It'll be part market, part collective."

He smiled ruefully at my enthusiasm.

"Then I won't be a bureaucrat anymore. I'm still terrified of the prospect of ownership. Even now, after all the months of thinking, planning and deciding."

"Why do you think you can save Africa?"

"I don't. I think it can save me."

"How?"

"Rescue me from a life of small meaningless gestures, or an obsession with the inconsequential. The lines there are drawn too clearly, too boldly to be ignored. I've found meaning living on the edge of what's left of the future."

"The future!" He laughed brusquely. "You talk of com-

puters and satellites in America, and we can't provide electricity to power the whole country yet."

"The only thing Africa has left is the future," I insisted.

"But it matters whether we stumble or walk into it," he
said pointedly. "I will help you buy your land. Although I
don't know what difference it will make, how much change
what you want to do will bring. I will help you to buy your
land."

"Thank you, Alhaji," I said, leaning forward to kiss him.
He held me, drew my face close to his and said, "After all
these years I still do not know you. You are a strange
woman. You want no husband and will not let me give you a
child. Will you ever marry?" he asked, pressing me closer to
him even as I grew rigid in response to his question.

"I don't know. It's not important to me. Not now anyway," I said, and relaxed against him as I promised, "But if I
have a child—when I have a child, Alhaji—it will be yours."

I'll be going to the States in a few months, as part of a
delegation to seek funds for special women's projects from
private philanthropic agencies. My supervisor in the ministry has already told me I can spend up to six weeks there.
Crystal. Aisha. I haven't seen them in years. But in my
apartment I have copies of both Crystal's books. She used to
send me long letters with articles from the *Times* stapled to
them that gave me a sense of what was happening in the
States, and articles on whatever country I was in, scribbling
across the top, "How much of this is true?" or "Does this
sound like anyplace you know?"

But Aisha sends recipes, of all things—recipes clipped
from women's magazines. Recipes for timesaving dishes
that require a minimum of effort and ingredients, along
with articles on the latest diet fad, writing in the margin, "I
tried it and it doesn't work."

When they finished building the house in New Jersey, she
sent me pictures of it, one with her and the children standing in front of the house, one with Rasheed, her and the

kids. Tameka, her head wrapped in a long, flowing scarf, stood slightly apart from the others, although Aisha's hand rested on her shoulder. The day I received the pictures I studied them long after I finished the letter. Beside Tameka, Aisha was plump, indecipherable. Unlike Crystal's letters—long, analytical, short stories really, that give the impression of leaving nothing out—Aisha's are crammed with details of everyone's life except her own. Her children's grades, illnesses, punishments, Rasheed's moods, projects, her mother's health, all unfold with cataloglike efficiency.

The letters are hurriedly scribbled on legal-size yellow paper, and they trail off at the end into an incomprehensible blur of words; each ends with the request that I answer her "as soon as possible." Responding to what is a plea for help and understanding, I answer Aisha's letters the same day they arrive.

It's 8:30 A.M., and from my office window that opens on the square I smell the cleansing odor of dew still moist in the air. I like to measure a country, a city, by the way morning arrives. The vigorous crowing of a cock in someone's backyard, the palm trees promising forever, the chant of young girls selling bread, the skyscrapers still too few to obstruct the sun, all imbue daybreak with more possibilities here, I believe, than anywhere else. The city's not yet fully awake, but the buses have been streaming in since dawn, filled mostly with women from the nearby townships. They descend on the capital six days a week to set up vending stalls in the market, to work as domestics or to pace the streets selling lace shawls. Those not lucky enough to catch one of the few, irregularly running buses walk six miles. A seemingly endless line of women stretches along the highway that ends in the capital. They come with their babies on their backs, baskets of produce on their heads, accompanied by daughters and some sons pressed into service by the requirements of survival. Some mornings they enter the city singing, to combat the onslaught of fatigue, their voices joined, giving each one more strength. Oddly enough, some of the songs they sing are war chants, rousing the morning's silence, informing the city, "We are here."

I watch the streets below me filling like a stage. It's 8:40 and the whites, who still control the nation's economy despite "majority rule," stride as confidently as ever past the women, on their way to air-conditioned offices. The educated, suited and tied Africans, who for the first time work with the whites, pass the women, too, rushing past them as though the women's cast-off clothes, their children's unwashed faces, their inability to read, their by-foot migrations at dawn and dusk are a contagious disease. Most people viewing the drama that unfolds in the seconds it takes these men to pass the women would consign the women to the role of Greek chorus. But having watched this scene unfold so many times, I know it's the women who, though unschooled, wrote the play. They gave birth to those men. And because the revolution has not yet come, the women are still the bridges the men cross to enter buildings the women pass with bowed heads.

It is nine o'clock and I turn from the window and in a last quick gulp finish my tea and head for my first meeting of the day.

Margaret Mubi removed the cigarette from her lips and placed it in an ashtray on her desk. Her brows were furrowed in obvious concern as she read my report. Reading the report the way she does everything, with her whole body, her small eyes devoured each line. Her face was a barometer of reactions as her hands neatly folded the pages over and she shifted position in her swivel chair, several times as she read. She's a pixie of a woman in size who has the demeanor of a general. Watching her reach for the cigarette, sliding it effortlessly between her lips, I remember the first time we met. I'd been given a letter of introduction to Margaret by a friend in Kenya who had met her at a conference. When I decided to come here, I wanted the name of someone who could help me if I decided to stay.

The day Margaret interviewed me, I watched her read over the letter of introduction and my attached résumé, much the way she sits reading the report now. On that day, she read the letter, scanned the résumé, folded them both and handed them back to me, her face revealing nothing. Then she leaned back in her chair and looked at me as though trying to spot a weakness.

"Since independence, this country has been flooded with foreigners from all over the continent and the world," she finally said. "Some come to exploit us, some to enrich themselves in some way on the bounty of our freedom. Only a few, a very few, have come to offer what they have to the new struggle we face." She paused to let her words sink in. "Why are *you* here? What do *you* want?"

"I'm not here for a job," I told her. "I'm here to make a certain kind of life for myself." Then I told her about what I'd done in Egypt, and in Kenya, and why it's the only kind of work I want to do. "If you don't hire me I won't leave the country," I assured her. "I'll find work. I'll make my life here with or without you."

Smiling, she asked, "Do you speak any of our languages?"

"Not today. But I will in three months." She hired me to work with the Women's Ministry, which at that time was still in the planning stages.

Margaret is a widow whose husband, a colonel in the liberation army, died of a heart attack three days after the independence celebrations. "Can you believe it?" she asked one evening as we drove home after work. "Wounded five times in the war. But he lived to die of something like that." We had stopped at a light and Margaret said quietly, "I thought if he could survive the fighting somehow he'd be safe from everything else."

"Do you think his death less noble because it didn't come during the struggle?"

"For a long time, yes, I did."

Everyone who knows Margaret has a favorite anecdote that summarizes how unusual she can be. It wasn't long after we met that I began to collect my own store of folklore. We had agreed to have dinner one evening in a hotel still patronized largely by whites. When I entered the lobby I found Margaret loudly upbraiding an African waiter. The man was shaking in fear, about, any moment it seemed, to fall on his knees in supplication. "Remove that uniform because I'm going to have your job," Margaret loudly warned him. When she spotted me she motioned for me to follow her and strode toward the dining room. When we were seated, she explained that the waiter had assumed that since she was standing in the lobby she was a prostitute rather than a patron and had threatened to have her arrested if she didn't leave the hotel. The manager came on the scene just as Margaret opened her wallet to show the waiter her government ID. The manager apologized profusely but Margaret told him she wanted the man fired. As we sipped drinks and waited for our orders to arrive, the manager came over to our table and informed Margaret that the waiter had been dismissed. When I protested, she said, "Don't you know that I could have demanded that he be banned from working in any hotel in the country? He will find another job. But he will never again automatically assume that an African woman in a place like this is a prostitute."

Now, Margaret laid the report on her desk and asked, "What are we to make of this?"

"That perhaps our emphasis at this stage is off track. Frankly, I found a logic in their statements that was hard to refute. We want to stamp out polygamy and bride price. Yet these women still can't read, their labor is backbreaking and their diets are inadequate. What they told me is that those are women's issues too. And they said we should deal with them first."

"But those problems are the province of other ministries. The prime minister did not give us a mandate to deal with those things. And besides, bride price oppresses the women, and not only in a philosophical sense. Look at the inheritance laws—they can work the land but not own it. And bride price symbolizes an attitude that the men have toward the women, that the women's families share, that the women themselves hold on to. An attitude that says they are chattel to be bought, forfeited, bargained over. As long as they see themselves as property, they'll never have any rights of their own."

"I know, I know the tribal laws, the noninheritance customs. But until we can make changes in these basic aspects of their lives, the women wonder, and I feel rightly, how will we change custom which isn't retaught as easily as a school is built or a well is dug?"

"In reality the women are indicting the other ministries," Margaret said.

"The women are indicting us all."

"You're arguing for the irrelevance of this ministry, it seems."

"No, I'm arguing for a reevaluation of what we do and how we do it. Why can't we work *with* the Ministry of Rural Development, the Ministry of Education, instead of competing with them? We've got to earn the trust of the women. We can't impose our notion of progress on them and expect them to shower us with gratitude."

"Do you know how difficult it will be to get three ministries to work together?"

"I can imagine."

"Politically it will be nearly impossible; logistically, a nightmare."

"But it's the only way."

"Sometimes I think the decision to give women a ministry of our own was mere shrewdness on the part of the prime minister," Margaret said with a shake of her head. "Whatever happens, no one can question his commitment. All he has to do is point to us."

"But will he back us all the way? That's the real question," I asked.

"With the sabotage attempts, he'll hardly have time to consider a proposal such as you're making now. A curfew is being considered."

"I heard."

"Let me read the report again and we'll map out a strategy."

Later Margaret came into my office and told me, "I may have sounded harsh about your report, like I was dismissing it. I wasn't. It's just that I know those women you talked to. They are my mother, my grandmother, my aunts. And they are at once the most conservative and potentially radical force in the country. They want change, but they fear it. In their hearts, they want a revolution that will alter the shape of their lives but not its meaning. But that's not the revolution we fought for."

I knew of Margaret's role as a commander. Margaret, like most of the women in the ministry, had been a soldier, was a "comrade" in the Party groomed to lead during the harsh years of war.

"How did you decide to join the fighting?" I asked.

"In those days there was no other choice. I crossed the border into Zambia to get training. Then I was assigned to a camp, where eventually I became a commander. So many of the men had been captured and were in prison at that time, many of the camps had women leaders."

"How did you feel when you had to kill?"

"It surprised me how quickly I got used to handling a gun. How it became part of me. I slept with it at my side. Even when I bathed in the river it was not far away. But when the fighting stopped, I was glad to give it up. But the men held on to their weapons, hid caches of them in the bush as if the guns contained some kind of magic and if they had to relinquish them, they themselves would be useless."

"What was it like in the camps?"

"Bullets didn't kill most of the people. In the camps we were burying thirty people a day who died from malnutrition. Yet we were all heroes and heroines then. And the survival of a nursing mother was a victory of sorts. We were partners with the men in a way we may never be again."

"Everyone was a hero?"

"The men listened to us. In the camps they did women's work if necessary. We performed the jobs of men. Our biggest task was just to survive. And in trying to do that, we honored each other as equals."

"The women asked me when the revolution would come to their villages."

"You should have told them it will arrive there when it arrives in the rest of the country."

"That's not a politically sound answer," I chided her.

"No, but it is an answer we won't have to pay for years from now. I helped make the revolution, so I know its limits, its possibilities. Or would you have me tell them the truth— that maybe their grandchildren will be fetching water from a stream four hours away or that the revolution will probably make life better for a few of us but certainly not all, because there won't be a true revolution here, that the I.M.F. and the multinational companies won't allow it. And that everybody who is anybody in the Party traded the idea of revolution for shares in one of the mining companies long before the shooting stopped. No, I'll never tell them the truth. None of us will. But my answer at least promises hope. And it's the only answer those women deserve."

We parked on an embankment off the highway across from the land. Since our last trip out to look at the plot, the eight 2-acre sections had been fenced in. Several soldiers with rifles slung over their shoulders casually patrolled the area.

"Soldiers *and* fences?" I asked, looking across the highway.

"The squatters have gotten completely out of hand," Cecil Witherspoon, the real estate agent, told me. "They get on a piece of property and there's no getting them off. I've lost more than my share to them. I've a few well-placed friends in the government so I gave them a call."

As Witherspoon walked around to my side of the car to open the door, I wondered if this land would have been guarded if all those who had purchased the plots had not been upper- and middle-level civil servants. Helping me out and holding me by the elbow, Witherspoon reminded me, "I could've easily sold this plot long ago. But since you asked me to hold it until you returned, that's what I did."

From behind my sunglasses I looked at the man's overeager face and said, "Thank you for your patience, Mr. Witherspoon. It means a lot to me." When we crossed over to the other side of the highway, we passed a young soldier dressed in a uniform that was still freshly creased. But he held his rifle carelessly, as though indifferent to the meaning of the weapon. As the soldier opened the locked gateway of the fence, Witherspoon continued, "Land's worth more than money. In this country today, if you've got no land you've got no future."

Once inside the fence, I looked around and saw only sky, a few trees. I removed my sandals and walked barefoot across the earth. Lifting my skirt, I kneeled and grabbed a fistful of soil, squeezed it and watched it filter through my fingers.

"Will you build on it?" Witherspoon asked, eyeing me with the skeptical glance that had tried so often in the weeks of our business association to size me up once and for all.

"For a while, I just want to own it." This idea intrigued but didn't impress him, for he observed with a broad sweep of his hand, "You're lucky there're soldiers guarding all these plots."

"Lucky to have bought this plot instead of some other, or lucky not to be a land-hungry peasant?"

"Both," he said flatly, hoisting up his pants, patting his stomach. "Land's no good unless you use it. Grow on it. Build on it."

"Mr. Witherspoon, I bought this land so I could do something useful, something necessary."

"Well, if that's what you want, it is your land." He shrugged.

"Yes, it is my land," I repeated, only because I liked the sound of the words.

I scooped up more soil and smelled the mixture of chemicals, manure and seedlings. Throwing the soil toward the sky, as it rained down upon me I laughed, a brazen, shocking laugh that shook my body and echoed across the field. And closing my eyes, I hugged myself in congratulation. The moist soil had nearly penetrated the skin of my legs and knees. I could have stayed there all day. I could have slept quite happily on my land that night, sheltered only by an approving sky. Instead I rose and began to run, my feet digging into sod, rocks, clumps of grass burrowing between my toes. I ran until breathless. I felt my heart leaden and throbbing in my chest.

Slumping on the ground, I laughed again, even as between gasps I took in huge gulps of air. I imagined the stalls the women would build and heard their voices as they bargained, bought and sold. And because I was still unsure and afraid, I hugged myself again. For in that place at that moment, there was no one else to do it. The smell of the earth floated up to my nostrils from my fingertips. My tears and laughter became a song that I listened to until I felt calm and less afraid. And when I was ready, I stood up and walked very slowly back to my sandals and put them on.

Cecil Witherspoon stood smoking a cigarette and didn't try to hide his astonishment as, dirt smudged and rumpled,

I neared him. Silently we walked through the fence and across the highway to the car. And as we drove away, I turned in my seat and looked back at my land and then at the memory of it all the way back home.

Tameka

WHEN I came into the living room, even though I couldn't see him, I could hear daddy's breathing. I dropped my school books on the sofa and listened to all the sounds filling the room. There was the rain. But it wasn't really the rain I heard so much as the whistling, gliding sound of tires driving over shiny, slippery streets. The rain always seems to me like a feeling. The kind of feeling that makes me want to get under the covers of my bed or sit on the sofa next to mama after Malika and Muhammad have gone to sleep, and tell her everything I did in school.

I couldn't see daddy but I knew where he was. His snores told me that. He spends a lot of every day now sitting in a corner of the living room in his wheelchair, real far away from the sofa, the stereo, the bookcases, our toys—everything that makes us want to come into the room. The corner where he sat was dark—darker even than the rest of the room, which was as gray as the sky outside. And as I went over to him, like I do every day when I come home, his snoring didn't scare me because it was a sound that reminded me how he used to be.

I pushed the wheelchair out of the corner, where it seems daddy doesn't so much sit as hide. He doesn't look as big as he used to, but whenever I push the wheelchair, I know he still is. When he sleeps in his chair, his shoulders and arms, all of him seems to curl in on him, the way a baby sleeps. I've learned the meaning of the phrase "dead weight" from pushing my daddy out of different corners in the house. I first heard the word from my friend Imani. She's always showing off by using big words. The wrong way. When I heard her call somebody that, I looked the word up in the dictionary in the school library and I thought about how it feels to push daddy in his wheelchair. Then I closed the dictionary real fast, like I'd been looking up something that might get me in trouble. But I've never said the word out loud. The "dead" part scares me too much.

Daddy's got one of those little buttons you can push to make his chair go like a car. But I like to push him, because then I can be close to him. I can smell the Dial soap on the back of his neck and look at him up close and see how even though he's old, his skin is soft with hardly any lines at all. I can touch him this way, too, by pushing him, touch his shoulders or his good arm. I'm the only one he doesn't mind coming close. He kind of gets smaller, almost like he's shrinking, when Tariq, Malika and Muhammad want to come to him. Like he's scared of them. So now they're scared of him too. And they act all the time like he's not there, especially when he's in the same room with us. But when mama has to do something for him—put his chair in the little elevator that takes him upstairs, or help him into the bathroom, or even one time I passed their bedroom and saw mama on her knees tying his shoes—whenever mama comes toward him, daddy's body gets bigger, fills up the chair, and he tries to sit up straight as he can, and it's like his body is saying, "I can do it myself," even though he knows he can't.

He didn't wake up as I pushed him, so he faced the over-stuffed green chair that he used to sit in after dinner or when he read stories to us. One time, but this was a long time ago now, Malika busted into the living room and found daddy just sitting in the chair and asked what he was doing. He looked at her and said, "I'm thinking, honey. Just thinking." And from then on we started calling the chair the thinking chair. And sometimes when he wasn't home, me and Tariq would play a game we named the "thinking game." We would take turns sitting in the chair and give clues to what was on our mind. We never get to play that game too much now because mama's always saying she'll punish us if we play in daddy's chair. We haven't played that game in a long time. And daddy hasn't sat in the chair since he got sick.

So I sat in it and looked at my daddy sleeping. His head was crooked over real far onto his right shoulder, and a thin thread of spit was dripping from between his lips. His hair is all white now. But except for the change in his hair, he looks almost the same as before. "Before" is usually as far as I get when I'm thinking like this. Only once or twice did I get as far as "before the stroke."

Daddy's eyes started fluttering. His fingers began twitching as he woke up. And his breathing got softer. I knew that in a minute he would be awake. I thought about moving out of his chair. But I'm his favorite and I knew he wouldn't be mad. So when he finally opened his eyes, which were all sleepy, looking like they really didn't want to open, I smiled and said "Hello."

He can't say but a few words now and hello is one of them. There's a lady that comes and helps him learn how to talk again and they worked on that word for a long time. But instead of saying hello, he smiled at me with his eyes. He would've stretched if he could have moved his left side. But it's paralyzed. So he just sort of shifted in the chair, moving his right arm and leg. Twice a week mama takes him to the hospital, where he does exercises that are supposed to make his body good again. He's supposed to do some of the exercises at home, but he never does. The bad side of his body is shriveled up and thin. And the good side—the arm and leg he can use—is stronger than ever. So, with his good hand daddy wheeled closer to me. He put the same hand on my cheek, squeezing it between his thumb and index finger.

"Hi daddy," I said again. And he opened his mouth and a sound came out. So soft I could hardly hear it. He was saying hello. Then daddy sank back into the chair like saying it had made him real tired, and he sat and watched me watching him.

I showed him a geography test that I got an A on. And then I sat on a hassock in front of him and read passages from the Qu'ran. And as I read, I thought about mama, upstairs in the bed asleep. I knew that without even looking, and my brothers and sisters in the basement playing. And so I read to daddy and felt glad that then, anyway, he belonged just to me.

We'd only been in the new house a little while when daddy got sick. Mama said he was at his store in Brooklyn unpacking a box of wrenches when he just fell on the floor. They had to operate on him and us kids didn't get to go to the hospital to see him at first. And when we did get to see him, he didn't know us. Aunt Crystal came and stayed with us for a while when daddy was in the hospital. But mama told us not to tell daddy or we'd go on punishment. Aunt Crystal took mama to the store and watched us when she had to go to the hospital and sometimes she and mama would sit in the living room until one o'clock in the morning drinking tea and talking. The whole time Aunt Crystal was here they'd do that every night. Like it was something special, and all they were doing was talking. About old-timey people and places they knew before I was born.

I'd climb out of bed and sit at the top of the stairs and listen to them. Mama talked to Aunt Crystal in a different way than she talked to anybody else. It's not that she was talking more, it was like she was talking because she wanted to. Kinda like she talks to me and the other kids sometimes. But I don't think I ever saw her talk to daddy like that. You know, like me and Imani talk, like it's not so important what we're saying as that we're saying it to each other. One night

I thought about all that and started crying right there on the steps, started crying so loud I was scared they'd hear me and went back to my room to bed. That night I slept with the light on, like I used to do when I was little.

Anyway, daddy finally came home and seemed like he was mad all the time. We had to be real quiet. No running in the house, no playing anywhere except the basement. Back then daddy didn't want to hardly do nothing. Just stare out the window all day long. And for the first time we were scared of him. When it was time to go to bed, didn't nobody want to hug him like we used to. The others were scared to be first, so I had to do it first every night. All four of us would be lined up beside his chair. And it felt like daddy was made of stone. He'd never try to kiss you back. Just let you hold him, but like he didn't really want to. And I don't remember daddy ever smiling back then. He don't smile *that* much now. And never at mama.

It was a long time before we all had dinner together when daddy came home from the hospital. At first he'd eat all by himself in the bedroom. Eat breakfast, lunch and dinner there. But the lady who comes to teach daddy how to talk again said he should start eating with us. So one night we were sitting at the table and all of us—even Muhammad—were real quiet. Mama blessed the food and then we all started eating. But daddy just looked at his food like something was wrong with it. Then he looked around the table at the rest of us. He picked up his fork with his good hand and tried to pick up his knife with his bad hand but it fell on the floor. Mama got him a new one and then she started cutting up his meat. When she finished he looked at her like she'd done something wrong and he picked up the plate and threw it on the floor.

Then his face got that look on it like Muhammad's gets when he wants to cry but he don't want nobody to know it. He turned around and wheeled himself into the living room. Mama bent down on the floor and cleaned up the mess and she went to the sink and stood there with her back to us. She started to go into the living room and then she looked like she was scared and came back to the table and sat down and finished her dinner. Now most of the time he eats by himself, shakes his head no when mama asks if he's ready to eat. Goes into the kitchen and fixes something for himself and leaves the biggest mess you ever saw, since he can't get around much or really use both hands.

Mama's started sleeping all the time, going around the house in her robe. Seems like even when she's awake she's asleep. Daddy sits in a corner of the house looking out the window or just staring. I've heard so many big words since daddy got sick—"unpredictable behavior," "therapeutic recovery"—I just listen to the words and watch the reaction of whoever hears them and what kind of voice whoever says them uses, and after a while I know what they're saying, what it all means. I guess daddy is getting a little better. 'Cause now he will at least try to talk to me. Nobody else, though. Tariq is jealous. But I tell him right now daddy can only do one thing at a time and maybe right now he can only love one of us at a time. Tariq hit me in the stomach when I told him that. And I didn't even hit him back, 'cause I know daddy's gonna love us all again one day.

Rasheed

I CAN see Aisha ironing clothes. She's humming as she folds the clothes and stacks them in a wicker basket on the floor. My tongue is thick and heavy, all bunched up in my mouth. I've got a headache and I want an aspirin. But that means getting her attention, and to get her attention, I have to try to speak. I'll release a sound so strange, my own heart will pound at the sound of it. And if it interrupts a silence, as it would now, my voice will make me forget what I wanted to say. I could write out what I want on the pad on the coffee table, but nobody can read the letters I make with my left hand and I'm ashamed every time I have to write. So I'll sit in this chair instead, and will my body into stillness, to dull the band of pain tightening around my head.

I never wanted to speak to her as much as I do now. But I don't even know what I'd say to her if I could talk. Before, she was the one who asked for words. But I built this house, provided for her and our children, worked hard in my business to become a man in my and everyone else's eyes. This has been my language—all those things were my words— and sometimes it's like she never heard any of it.

In the beginning I was a middle-aged man who had married a child. Now I'm an old man, a crippled old man who

207

has a young wife. It's now that she'll leave me. Just like I saw in the dream. She thinks I don't trust her. But what it really is, only I know. I don't trust the happiness she's given me. I watched her make doll clothes and stuffed toys for Tameka and Malika, watched my sons cling to her skirts. Each child revealed some part of her that without that child, I might not have ever seen.

But she changed. The children, my attempts to guard her from the world, her own innocence—none of it stopped her from growing up and out of my hold.

The week before I had the stroke, she told me she was going back to school. When I said I wouldn't give her money to pay for any classes, she told me she had money of her own from selling her wall hangings. "The children are all in school now. There's no need for me to stay at home anymore." "You can't stop me," she said. Then after I had the stroke she came to the hospital and told me, "I said you couldn't stop me. You proved you could." She's no longer a child. Never will be again. And yet I loved her as a child. I don't know if I can love her as a woman. Wondering if I can only makes the pain worse, sets it traveling from my temples, stabbing me in the veins of my neck so sharply I can feel my eyes closing. Finally I raise my hands to get her attention and open my mouth to speak. . . .

Aisha

IT'S got so I can't even make salat. I lay in bed while the children are at school and nearly get a headache trying to remember how to let Allah touch me. All that faith I had, and now I can't even remember the words. I wanted to pray so bad the other day, I started crying. Walking through the house, cleaning up, cooking, taking care of the kids and tears just streaming down my face. But I knew Allah heard the prayer I couldn't speak, heard it inside my tears.

I go to the mosque and it don't mean what it used to. The mosque hasn't changed. The faith is the same. It's me. And since I can't pray, I can't think of anything to say to Rasheed, 'cause it's from Allah, anyway, that I'd get the words to heal my husband and free myself.

Ruth MacMillan

As I watched her pouring tea, I tried to guess her age. It's hard to tell, not only because of the long head covering she wears and the ankle-length dresses, but because there is so much she holds back. She must have been quite lovely in her teens, in the years before she began editing herself so ruthlessly. The absence of makeup seems just to enhance a natural softness and allure in her face of which she is obviously unaware. She handed me a cup of tea and stirred sugar into her own, then let it sit untouched on the coffee table.

"Mrs. Ali, to tell you the truth, I'm making very little progress with your husband. It's almost as if he doesn't want to regain his speech." I stopped and waited for a response from her, but she said nothing. She merely sat on the sofa as though summoned to the principal's office, her head slightly bowed, her demeanor indifferent and strangely defiant.

"Does he try to talk to you and the children?"

"Not much."

"Sometimes it's good, we find, to make the patient's spouse and family an integral part of the process of rehabilitation." She looked at me curiously. "What I'm suggesting is that in addition to the sessions with me, *you* could work with your husband as well."

"But I don't know how," she said, her voice rising in panic.

"We have a course for spouses to take that teaches them how to teach," I assured her. But I wasn't surprised to see her eyes widen in terror.

"Even before the stroke, we never talked much. And when we did, he did most of the talking. I just don't think it would do much good."

"I'm going to ask you a question that in my capacity as speech therapist I have no right to ask, but the answer to it may help me. Do you love your husband?" Her face was passive, absolutely barren of clues to a possible answer.

"Does he love you?"

"One time he did. I don't know about now."

"This rehabilitative process can be difficult for marriages. I've seen it destroy some and make others stronger. You may feel the need to talk to someone professionally. This could help both of you."

"I wouldn't know what to say to my husband, even if he was ready to listen. I wouldn't know how to tell a stranger that I don't know what I feel. That sometimes I don't have any feelings at all."

I was relieved by the passion in her voice and asked, "Won't you just try to reach your husband?"

But she insisted, "I can't. Not now. I just need time to figure out what I'm gonna tell him, and what it is I want him to say."

Neil

SO this is it. We are not charmed, not special. And it will be as hard for us as for everybody else. Tonight we are celebrating our third wedding anniversary. "The bad times" are over. That's what I say though I know it isn't really true. Just last month I dragged Crystal home early from a party when she seemed to be enjoying too much the conversation of a man who had the look of seduction on his face. I appeared behind her like a ghost, bearing her coat, saying, although it was only eleven o'clock, "Honey, I've got a big day tomorrow and I want to turn in early." She showed no surprise, and in the elevator down to the lobby merely said, "Nice party." Once in the car, however, sitting beside her, I pounded the steering wheel with my fists, yelling, "I still don't trust you. I don't know if I ever will again."

I felt her fingers tracing the outline of my ear. "You will trust me again one day," she assured me. "We will have been together so long, there will be so many other sins to overlook, that trusting me will be easy and you will wonder why you ever doubted." I placed my palm over her fingers, discovering them in a slow entwining of our hands.

"Maybe I want to lose you after all. I can't really find any other reason for what I'm doing," I said.

She turned my face to hers and kissed me fiercely. When she finished she rested her head on my shoulder as her hands played around the edges of my fingers still clutching the steering wheel and said wearily, "Let's go home, where we belong. Let's go home, Neil, where we will be safe."

When I left her I spent a year and a half in San Francisco making a documentary about a group of Vietnam vets. And Crystal wrote me letters each month that I didn't answer. I dated a succession of women, none of whom really interested me, all of whom I chose because they reminded me of something about my wife.

I hadn't seen her in over a year when she came out. And yet when I looked at her, I still saw what she had done to me. She was settling herself on the sofa in my apartment, and I realized that I was nervous. The palms of my hands were sweating, and I was dancing restlessly around the room. "I'd offer you something but I haven't got much here," I said from the kitchen.

"Don't bother, I'm fine," she said politely. In the living room I sat down across from her and asked, "Why did you come?"

She didn't answer immediately, sat picking nonexistent lint from her skirt, examining the carpet, and then she finally looked at me, saying, "Since I know you can't, I won't ask you to forgive me."

"Even you haven't got that much nerve," I said, feeling it all bubbling up inside me. And before I knew it I was standing up, looking down at her, shouting, "You know why I hate you? Because you make me want to use my fists on you like my father did with my mother. You make me feel like there's something wrong with me because I won't."

"Neil, you never gave me a chance to explain. You just left."

"You left me long before I left you, and besides, you took away any reason for me to stay."

"Once you told me that nobody else mattered," she cried. "Maybe not for you. But for me, my father mattered, my brother too. What they think of my life meant more to me than I knew."

"Did you find them where you were looking?"

"Do I deserve that?"

"Did I deserve what you did?"

"You never lost a night's sleep. It was only me who was questioned, who forfeited, in the eyes of others, everything I am."

"Did they deny you *everything* you are, Crystal? I didn't want you because of that. I wanted you because of everything else. And don't talk to me about loss; you exacted your price from me."

She stood before me more vulnerable than I had ever seen her, clutching her bag and her jacket, yet ready, I could tell, at any moment to let them drop to the floor. I grabbed her, pulling her into my arms. And in my arms she was silent, her eyes closed tight, her breathing coming in small rapid bursts.

I opened her blouse, pushed her onto the sofa, and forced her legs apart with my knee, taking her the way I imagined those other men had, like a stranger who wanted everything she had because I knew it didn't belong to me. Even then she said nothing, just gave herself with a trust I had never earned from her before.

I took her again, and again. And when I was through, I couldn't look at her. She lay on the sofa, her clothes and hair rumpled, the odor of our bodies all over her like a stain. I couldn't look at her, so I asked her to leave. She gathered her things and told me as she headed for the door, "If it makes any difference, I love you. Before, it was me I didn't care for very much."

Nothing was the same after she left. My film was finished. But I delayed my return to New York as long as I could. On the plane I resolved to check into a hotel when I got to the city. But at the airport I flagged a taxi and heard myself give the driver the address of our apartment. When I opened the door with my key, I saw Crystal rocking gently in the antique rocker Carla gave us as a wedding gift. The curtains were drawn. The room was quiet. And Crystal was sitting in the dark.

Soon after I moved back home, she got pregnant. It was then that I was gripped by the feeling of melancholy that sometimes still holds me. One night as I was rubbing oil on her stomach to prevent stretch marks, I told her that I kept waiting to be more happy, more content. She just told me, "Neil, there isn't any more. There's you, me and the baby. That's all there is. Everything else is a riff, an improvisation on those three notes." She lost the child, miscarried in the fifth month, and though we never said anything, we were both relieved. Crystal had in fact never mentioned children, and unlike other expectant mothers had not worried over a room, clothes, baby-sitters. There won't be any children. We decided that.

This didn't please Carla very much when I told her.

"It's not because of the race thing, is it?" she asked, looking more surprised, disappointed, even, than I had expected. That's how she talks now. "The race thing. The nuclear thing." This linguistic change is the result, I can only conclude, of her affair with a thirty-two-year-old painter who shares the beachfront house in Ensenada that she's been renting for the past year. I sat watching her prepare gazpacho, sitting in the kitchen of the small but still impressive house when she asked this and I told her, "No, mother, it's not the race thing."

"Well, what is it then?" she pressed on in that insistent, prying voice she uses more and more now, as if determined to get everything she thinks the world owes her.

"We just want each other. Just doing that properly has been hard enough. Does that make any sense?"

"Of course it does." She smiled and set a bowl before me and poured the mixture from the blender. She poured the rest of the gazpacho into her own bowl and sat down. "Anyway there's still time. How old is Crystal, anyway?"

Changing the subject, I asked, "Where's Cathy?"

"She drove to San Diego for the day to visit some friends."

For one of the few times in my life I didn't know what to say to my mother. It seems very hard to talk to her now, she's so effervescent, so open, bubbling over with self-discovery. The affair with the lawyer didn't last long. I hadn't expected it to. But this new woman, they've been together almost a year and a half. Cathy is attractive, blond and blue-eyed. She could as easily be a movie starlet or a Playboy bunny if you just considered her looks. But she has a doctorate from Berkeley. And whenever I talk to Carla now, I have to endure a discourse on psychology, politics or human nature, sparked by a conversation with her lover. Cathy just barely tolerates me and said once, "You are, after all, your father's son, and Carla told me all about him."

"You seem to forget I'm also my mother's child," I told her, a remark that, to my profound disappointment, did not move her a bit. So I feign acceptance, but refuse to believe my mother is a lesbian. Refuse even to use the word.

Since I couldn't think of anything to say I just watched her thumbing idly through a copy of *Newsweek* as she ate the soup. She no longer dyes her hair, so it's a curly mass of black and brown, gray and white that frames her face quite beautifully. I haven't seen her in makeup since she left Jacob. She pads around the house barefoot and virtually lives in jeans and poncho-type Mexican tops. The wrinkles and crow's-feet she once considered extinguishing with plastic surgery give her face a depth I thought I would never see in my mother. Now, to my surprise, she is actually radiant.

But my father hasn't fared quite so well. He's a drunk. And Carla and I—in fact, everybody who knows him—are all just waiting for him to slip into a coma or get killed while driving, as they say so euphemistically, under the influence. He had checked into a sanatorium a few weeks before my visit to Carla, but he'd done that before and then come out only to start drinking again.

I sat with him on the manicured grounds of the hospital

the day I last saw him and rubbed his shoulders, listening to him complain about the food, the doctors, the cost of the treatment. And when it was time for me to leave, he hugged me, saying, "I'd do it all over again, the right way this time, if I just knew how." I wonder more and more these days what we all will do to make it. How we all will find a way to be happy.

Crystal

IN DESPAIR as in love, we are above all else, alone. When he came back, I tried to apologize. He told me he didn't want an apology, he wanted the marriage he had expected.

"We'll pretend it never happened," he said with a nearly lethal calm. "That's the only way we can go on."

He refused to let me speak, denied the voice of my contrition. And now he reigns in our home as intrepid as some ancient conquistador. In denying my plea for forgiveness, he assures neither of us will ever forget. Words are my sacrifice, my salvation. But he has made me a prisoner of my deeds.

He told me, "I plan always to be with you. Otherwise I would not have come back." But I know that he will never be mine like before. And I am his more completely than I thought possible.

Last night as he lay upon me, spent, moist and warm with sweat, I felt him take leave, move into some astral zone outside my reach and longing. He journeyed away from me, even as he held me close. He does this at odd moments. Over dinner his voice trails off. He deliberately fails to finish a sentence. He has returned, only to disappear before my eyes. But how could I live with anyone now who knew me less than he?

I will never forget how he left. I woke up one morning and felt his side of the bed vacant, the sheets as chilly as a November wind. I let my hand outline the spot where his hips would have rested, had he been beside me. My hands played over the shadowy remnants of him, stale creases on a sky blue colored sheet. I knew he had left me but I got out of bed anyway because the horrible script I had written for us required me to do this, rather than lie in bed and wish for a quick, painless death, which is what I really wanted.

Only a few ties and belts graced the necks of the naked hangers on his side of the closet. He had thoroughly cleaned out his drawers. A few pennies, a rain-soaked book of matches and a business card remained inside his cedar chest as clues to his former presence.

And in the living room, on the coffee table, white and round as snowballs, sat six pieces of paper crushed in disgust by his hand. I found myself strangely grateful to see the papers, piled beside a huge shell we found on a beach in Puerto Rico. Falling on my knees before the papers, studying them as intently as I might, had I never seen such a configuration before, I reached out for them, opening first one and then all, as delicately as if they were closed, sleeping flowers. Each sheet was blank, except for the salutation "Dear Crystal" near the top. I pressed each sheet flat and studied the wrinkles and the words for a long time. And then I cried. The way no one thinks I am capable of. I nurtured the tears, encouraged them, in order to spark an ever greater outpouring. And in the middle of my tears I remembered that Neil had never seen me cry, and thought, "Maybe that is why he left me. He never saw me cry, and so could not know who I am."

I placed the papers in a drawer of my desk and went back to bed. I stayed in bed for a week, getting up only to go to the liquor store a block away and buy more bottles of rum and six-packs of Coke. I unplugged my phone, drank rum and Coke, threw up, and slept for a week. When I plugged my phone back in the first call I got was from Carla who asked me why Neil had left. I lied, telling her I didn't know, and then I hung up and unplugged the phone for two more days. Then I called Carla and asked her where Neil was. She said he'd made her promise not to tell me, then she gave me his address.

I wrote him on the third day of each month for over a year. And with the letters I purchased time. Everything costs. After a while, I was unperturbed by the fact that he did not answer the letters. I didn't write them to receive an answer. I wrote the letters for him to read. When I had constructed a lifeline from my coast to his, I went out to California to reclaim what we had once vowed to have.

My pregnancy surprised us both. I considered the prospect of motherhood with unequivocal dread. Still, I kept the baby. I assumed Neil wanted children, but as my pregnancy progressed and his anxiety increased, I felt my spirit and body rejecting the child and I wasn't surprised when I lost it. Two days after I came home from the hospital, a package arrived from Serena—a baby-sized dashiki and pants in African material. Both Neil and I felt guilty for weeks afterward, that we had not really wanted the child. We only wanted each other.

I am developing a screenplay under his tutelage, and I have finished a play as well that is going to be staged at the Women's Studies Center of an upstate college. Serena will be coming home soon.

My father and I are now reconciled, and for the first time Neil and I spent Christmas with my parents last year. The demands of sustaining his rejection of us aged my father terribly. And he seemed somehow disappointed that Neil was, in the end, so easy to like. I sensed that my father gave in to my mother's insistence on meeting Neil as a way to erase other sins of which he is more aware as he grows older.

I still think Neil's expectations are too high. He wants—demands—too much of me, of everything. He thinks life is how much you are awarded. But I know it's how much you can salvage and find, after you have looked longer and harder than you imagined possible.

I received a grant to support the work on my next book, which will contain a cycle of poems about women heroes. After reading an article in the *Times* about the wife of Nelson Mandela and an activist doctor, Mamphela Ramphela, both of whom have been banned by the South African government, I wondered: If I lived in South Africa today, would I find writing under a state of siege impossible or the only possible way out?

A WOMAN'S PLACE

(for Winnie Mandela and
Mamphela Ramphela)

how do you ban
a revolution?
admittedly the orders
six years for one
twenty (so far)
for the other
steal the words

theft witnessed
by a world patiently
compiling evidence

history
inevitable
long-suffering
will set the date
for the trial
and it will be sooner
than you think

and so
existence
becomes a manifesto
a war chant

A WOMAN'S PLACE

beating its own drum
in a dialect
that is warning
and inspiration

in the townships where
despair is supposed to be
the only seed that grows

for one—
day care
teaching someone to read
for the other—
a clinic
headquartered in the living room
free food dispensed
in the kitchen
the real revolution
is pretty boring
and it is the only thing left
that matters

what are words anyway
but a way to discover
what you can do
what is living
but the deed
finally done

Serena

THE apartment is just as I expected. The furniture —Danish modern, sleek and functional. On the wall behind the sofa there's a nude painting of Crystal. The planes of her body, the depths of her dark brown coloring, cast an aura of mystery over the room. The canvas, Neil told me, was done when they visited Paris last year and stayed with an old friend of his from the days when he'd lived there. The painting is as accurate as a photograph and it's hung so that it's the first thing you see entering the apartment. Shelves and shelves of books line the walls, ceiling to floor.

I've been in the States three weeks, but most of that time has been spent traveling with two other women from the ministry to Washington, Philadelphia, Chicago, San Francisco, looking for money to support women's health and educational projects. My vacation only started a few days ago. We raised some money, got some pledges, but not nearly as much as we had hoped. The usual sources have dried up, and what luck we had was with alternative foundations, underwritten by wealthy young men and women whose politics are left-leaning.

As I walked out of the tastefully decorated offices of project officers who had politely turned us down I remembered

the slew of clippings Crystal had sent me—editorials, car-
toons, articles—that detailed the political disagreements
between the prime minister and a former ally dismissed
from the government. It was always and only tribalism, the
articles implied, in a head-shaking tone that bemoaned the
current chaos and seemed to hint that maybe white rule
wasn't so bad after all. Then, too, the country isn't fashionable anymore. Not like the year immediately following the
end of the war. A small country in Central America that
recently threw out its U.S.-backed dictator now warms the
hearts of the nation's liberal left, gets most of their funds,
volunteers, and media attention.

"On the road in America," at the end of those days of 10
A.M. meetings and sometimes afternoon lunches and even
evening drinks with foundation officers, soaking in a warm
bath in my hotel room I tried to blot out the contradictions
of it all. Here I am, back in the States begging funds for a
sovereign black nation I consider home. And all the arguments about neocolonialism and how the West underdeveloped the rest of the world couldn't assuage my anger or
dissipate the feeling of vulnerability that crept upon me
almost as soon as I got off the plane at JFK.

In each city I took a day off from my schedule of appoint-
ments and meetings to ride the buses through the working-
class and poor neighborhoods. Listening to conversations,
measuring facial expressions, witnessing the dramas that
erupted over the correct fare, standing bunched between
passengers during the evening rush hour—all this informed
me of the mood of the country more precisely than anything
I read in the papers. While in Detroit, one day I went back to
my old high school and found it had been torn down. In its
place the city has erected a monstrous structure that sprawls
over two blocks, surrounded by high gates. Each entrance
to the building is patroled by a security guard. In the afternoon I sat in a McDonald's across the street, watching the
students leaving that building and board yellow buses or
walk in groups toward the corner. The students appeared

more knowing and at the same time more unaware than I was at seventeen. Watching a group of them come through the door, I wondered how their parents explain the world to them. I wondered if many of their parents know how to explain a phenomenon that baffles, ignores and conquers them in a hundred new ways every day.

A young girl stood in line waiting to order when a boy at a nearby table summoned her with lighthearted possessiveness: "Come here, bitch." The girl pouted, turning to him saying, "You gonna make me lose my place." And in the moments it took the girl to walk to his table, over her shoulder asking the man who stood behind her to save her place, my heart broke several times.

I had pitifully little to say to my parents except that I love them. I found no way to answer their obvious befuddlement over the life I've chosen. My father was forced into early retirement from the GM assembly line, and an expensive "recreational vehicle" sits in the driveway. Proudly, my mother showed me the inside of the van, which sleeps four, has a kitchen, shower and mock dining room. They spend a good part of the year now traveling all over the country, and one evening they showed me slides of a trip to Utah and Wyoming.

"I'm surprised you haven't gone and married one of them African men over there," my mother observed one evening as we sat together watching the news.

"Now and then I wonder if I'll ever marry. Most times I just don't wonder at all," I told her.

"We're not cut from the same cloth," she said in response, her eyes still on the screen.

"Thank God for that," I said.

She turned her glance sharply to me and I expected rebuke. Instead my mother only said, and with a smile that articulated more than her words, "Amen."

I've been with Neil and Crystal for almost a week. Neil, I discovered all over again. Before I left for Africa, Crystal arranged for the three of us to have dinner in Chinatown.

That was the only time I'd met him before. I was so genuinely surprised that Neil was white and at Crystal's apparent ease with him that I didn't really assess him very closely that evening.

But as I think back to that night now, I recall noticing in Neil that cheerful, casual confidence white men cultivate to take on and ensnare the world. Yesterday he left for West Virginia to look at some locations for a film he's directing. He's changed, I sensed that immediately, but it wasn't until we sat up one evening and talked a few nights after my arrival, long after Crystal had gone to bed, that my judgment was confirmed. We watched one of the late-night news programs and somehow ended up playing chess until two in the morning. We talked about food (he does most of the cooking), told anecdotes about our favorite cities, and I filled in the gaps in his knowledge about Africa and he told me about the parts of Europe I have yet to see.

"So what does seeing America again mean to you?" he'd asked.

"I'll be glad to get back to Africa where things make sense." I laughed. "My parents spend six months out of the year traveling from one end of the country to another, taking slides of the Grand Canyon and the Statue of Liberty. An article I read in some magazine the other day predicted a generation of blacks who will never know what it is to hold full-time jobs. My old high school has been rebuilt and looks like a prison. What am I to make of all this? Anything? Or nothing at all?"

"Probably both."

"Frankly, I feel like a foreigner."

"Accept the fact that you've been away too long to be anything else."

He doesn't seem to take as much for granted as I suspect he did before. There is a humility, a patience about him that makes him more interesting. He has suffered and his face holds shadows of everything he's learned. His jokes are biting but not bitter. He's too sure of himself, really, to give in to bitterness. After the game of chess we had two shots of brandy and I told him, "I think Crystal is an extraordinary woman, you know. I feel lucky that she's my friend."

"She is special," he agreed. "Being married to her is different, of course, than being her friend. It didn't turn out quite like I'd planned."

"What does?"

"Not much, that's for sure."

"Why didn't you divorce her?" I asked very carefully.

"Another woman might have loved me better. Maybe I could have loved someone else more. It's been ruthless sometimes, but it's been good. I didn't divorce her because I would not have wanted my life without her."

Despite all the years I've been away, my reunion with Crystal was rather subdued. She has the same face I've always known, although I did spot a few tiny gray hairs around the edges of her natural, as neat and closely cut as ever. I sat in the kitchen as she stir-fried some vegetables in a wok my first night back and she asked, "Did you miss Aisha and me?"

"No, not really. I always felt you. You and Aisha. There were times when I'd need to talk to one or both of you and I could almost conjure you right before my eyes. When you were going through all that ugliness with Neil right after you got married, and when Rasheed had that stroke, I'd dream about you and Aisha almost every night."

Crystal turned around and said, "I could sense you too. That's why sometimes I didn't write. After a while, I didn't need to. But I'm sure you missed America."

"How could I? I've seen America everywhere—in Nairobi, in Abidjan, in Cairo. I've seen it all over the continent in the young educated Africans sporting American tastes and clothes, in the teenagers aping the dances and hairstyles, the only things black America exports. How I could miss America when it's homogenized the world?"

"What's it been like to be a woman over there?" Crystal asked, turning off the wok and pouring two glasses of wine.

"Strange, I admit that. To the men, I remain a curiosity, but once I almost did marry."

"You mean that guy in Kenya, the editor of that newspaper?"

"Yes, Paul Mwangwa."

"I never quite understood what happened. You were living together and then the next thing I knew, you didn't write about him anymore."

"He was killed. He died in an explosion in the offices of his newspaper."

"Oh Serena, why didn't you tell me?"

"I couldn't. I couldn't stand to think about it, much less write to you and Aisha to recount the long sordid story of his harassment and death."

"He obviously meant a lot to you."

"He was one of the few men of action I've met in all the time I've been over there. I wanted to be part of his life because of what he stood for. He was a member of one of Kenya's 'first families.' After independence, Paul's oldest brother served in the new government. That was in the days when everyone thought African rule really meant power to the people. Other members of his family were appointed to the boards of the large British trading companies that controlled the economy. So Paul grew up materially comfortable and groomed to play a leadership role.

"His first act of rebellion was to attend the University of Nairobi, rather than go to Oxford or Cambridge. Next he decided to become a journalist rather than go into the management end of his family's coffee business. When we met, he was the editor of a newspaper that had been transformed by its new owners from a tabloid featuring mostly sex and crime to a journal that vocally criticized government policies and the opposition parties, and that took a militant position of advocacy. The circulation under Paul's editorship doubled.

"I met him when he came into the highlands with one of his reporters to investigate the famine there that the government was trying to cover up. I was working with a semi-permanent relief agency. We hadn't been able to get any of the other papers to run anything about the drought, the dislocations and the deaths. At first he'd drive up to see me and we'd just talk a lot about the situation in the country, politics and the future of the region. Then I started going into Nairobi to see him when I had time off. I met his friends —professors at the university, writers, politicians, lawyers, some of whom had already served time in detention for their views. And then he asked me to stay in Nairobi and I did, moving in with him. We'd sit up all night with his friends, talking, arguing, debating. His editorials came, in part, out of those sessions. I'd hear people on the bus talking about the paper, and the vendors couldn't keep copies of *The Kenyan Drum* in stock.

"But after the paper ran a series of editorials demanding an inquiry into the murder of one of the government's most consistent critics in Parliament, advertisers suddenly started pulling out. The owners ordered him to tone down the editorials, threatening to fire him if he didn't. One night he was run off the road and two men pulled him out of his car and beat him badly. Despite all this, Paul assigned two of his reporters to interview the MP's family and friends, and what they learned would have forced a formal inquiry. But Paul chose not to use the information. He and some of his friends had decided to try to raise the money to start their own paper.

"Paul was going to resign, but before he could, he went to the newspaper offices one night, opened a package addressed to him and it exploded in his face. Students from the university turned his funeral into a demonstration against the government. And then a few weeks later there was a coup attempt. The army killed scores of people rooting out those suspected of being involved. I was even questioned, because I'd known Paul, and because I knew his friends."

"And you still stay?" Crystal asked incredulously.

"Everything happened so fast, Paul's death really didn't strike me, the meaning of it, till months afterward. I had stayed on in his apartment to keep from falling apart. Finally I moved out, spent a couple of months with his sister, but I was under surveillance. A number of us who had known Paul were being watched. Finally I left Kenya. It's the only country I feel I can never go back to."

"So even after all this, the continent is home for you?"

"You know I've always felt being safe was a waste of time." I took a sip of wine and asked her, "What was it like when you went back to Winthrop for your reading that time?"

"I felt totally out of place."

"Why?" I asked, more than a little surprised by her conclusion.

"The students. They're scared to take a chance, think an original thought. For example, they've got this computer in the office of academic counseling that tells students who they are."

"Who they are? What the hell are you talking about?"

"They can find out from the computer the most lucrative careers, the graduate schools they should attend to prepare for those careers. They can map out a whole strategy for their lives without taxing their brains or imaginations." Crystal lit a cigarette and said, "They can find out who they should be by pushing a few buttons and staring at a screen."

"Isn't that called progress?"

"By some people," she replied pointedly.

"Well, what kinds of questions did they ask you?"

"They wanted a blueprint, a formula for becoming not good writers but hugely successful ones, with no mistakes and no need for second chances."

"Isn't that what kids always ask adults for, not just an answer but *the answer?*"

"Maybe, but when I asked my parents I didn't seriously expect them to know. These kids do."

"Who can blame them? They're scared the world's gonna

blow up before they can inherit it. They deserve an answer, I agree with them there. I just wish they'd ask different questions. Did you feel old?" I asked. "Seeing it all again?"

"You bet."

"Listen to us, we even *sound* old."

"Can you believe it?" Crystal asked. "I remember when we thought we were going to change the world. Now we're ready to turn it over to a bunch of kids we don't trust or understand."

"I'll never be ready to do that," I told Crystal firmly. "Never. Not here or anywhere else."

I had spoken with Aisha several times by phone since my arrival, and found her in those calls as elusive as she was in her letters. Then one afternoon I went out to visit her alone. And Aisha managed to say everything I needed to hear, when at the front door of her house she greeted me with a fierce, everlasting hug, whispering over and over, "I knew you'd come back one day. I knew you'd come."

Aisha's joy upon seeing me was so fervent that I began to suspect that happiness was a feeling she was in danger of forgetting. And so I hugged her tightly, for all the years I had been away, for the weeks I would be back, and for the future years we might be apart.

I had brought gifts for her children, drums for the boys and beads and dresses made of African material for the girls. They are sturdy, handsome kids who plied me with so many questions about Africa that Aisha laughed in exasperation and said, "For today, you belong to them."

And even when she drove me back to Crystal's, the kids wild and raucous in the back seat of the station wagon, we spoke mostly of minor things. Watching her navigate the car through the traffic or warn the children "for the last time" to be quiet, I saw in Aisha all her letters—all the words that seemed shrouded and unsure, come to life in her voice and on her face. There wasn't so much after all for us to say; the endurance of our concern had said most of it. Watching

Aisha, I discovered that we only needed to continue to be to each other what time and luck had made us.

And yet, I've never heard a silence quite like that of Aisha's house. The muteness of the house mocks the pictures that hang on the living-room walls and that sit on the mantelpiece, of smiling children, posed but still at ease, their faces expectant and bright. The next day Crystal and I went to see Aisha together. Even our own voices didn't give life to the house—Crystal's measured, controlled, as if afraid the room in which we sat was bugged; my own sounding too loud, bouncing off the hush around us. And Aisha's voice—a flat monotone, trembling in spite of itself. Since we finished lunch and moved from the kitchen into the living room, the three of us had sat, each one giving in to the quiet, satisfied just to be in the same room with the other two.

"How much longer will you be here?" Aisha asked.

"Another two weeks."

"Why are you going back?"

"Some people wear their countries best from a distance. I think I'm like that. It fits me better that way."

"Maybe one day I'll visit you," she said hopefully.

"I hope you do."

"How is Rasheed?" Crystal asked through a haze of smoke from her cigarette, her eyes piercing whatever defenses Aisha might try to erect.

"The same," she said.

I recalled seeing Rasheed being placed in a van in his wheelchair as Crystal and I drove up to the house. And as we got out of the car we saw Aisha standing at the front window watching the van drive him away for physical therapy. Aisha plied me with so many questions as we ate, nervously chattering in an agitated stream of conversation, that the question that mattered most to me was defeated in the onslaught. So now I asked, "How are you, Aisha?"

For the answer to my question she looked out the picture window that revealed a tree-lined street, benign beneath the afternoon May sun. Aisha looked out the window indifferently, as though she had not heard the question. Then she turned back to me and Crystal and said, "I haven't spoken to my husband in over three months. I'd never have believed I could live like this. You never know how much misery you'll face in this life, or what kind of peace you'll make with it."

"Why don't you teach him to talk again?" I asked. "Start with your name, teach him to say that and then teach him to say whatever else you need to hear."

"Sometimes I think he had that stroke on purpose, to make me stay the person I don't want to be anymore. Anyway, I've tried talking to him and I get no response. He hates me."

"He hates himself, because he's sick and mute," Crystal said.

"If you don't help him, what will you do?" I asked. "Unless you've got the courage to leave him, your only other choices are to help him or simply watch him wither, watch him die in front of your children. Will that free you?"

"You're calling me a murderer."

"I'm calling you a coward."

"There's not much difference."

"Aisha, he loved you the only way he knew how," I said. "Teach him how to love you the way you need."

"I don't know what I need."

"Yes you do," I shouted, grabbing her by the shoulders. She tried to remove my grip but I just held her tighter. "I used to think it was Rasheed you feared. Now I know it's you that scares you the most."

"I've tried," she blurted, choking on her words. "I've tried. Ask Crystal."

"Pretend I'm Rasheed and tell me everything you want to tell him."

"I can't."

"Tell me," I insisted, releasing her shoulders yet holding her hostage with my eyes.

Gazing at the carpet she said, "I wish you would touch me sometimes."

"Look at me," I asked her gently. "Look at me but see him." Raising her glance, Aisha bit her lip and said so softly I could hardly hear her, "I wish you would let me touch you. I want you to hold me. And I want you to let me go."

Aisha

IT'S been a long time since I've touched him. There've been nights I've lain beside him and swore I'd pay any price if he'd act like he loved me again. Then there were nights I lay in that same spot scared he might touch me, scared if he did I wouldn't know what to say, what to do or even what to feel. So when I finally touched him today, his hands got real stiff at first. Got cold, then clammy and then got stiff again. All the while I was getting up the nerve to do this, I'd been scared he might pull away from me, might not want me to lay a hand on him. But he let his hand rest in mine, just like that's where it belonged, like it had been lost all this time and finally found its way home. But I could still see suspicion in his eyes. He's been looking at me like that so long, I don't even think he could help it. His hands were telling me one thing, and his face something else. So I decided to listen to his hands. But for the longest time I just kneeled on the floor in front of him, stroking his hand; I couldn't even think of what to say. Then I let the calm I felt in him stop the sweat dripping under my arms, quiet down my stomach churning and contracting like I was giving birth again, just because I was gonna talk to my husband for the first time in three months.

Then I felt his other hand, the one that's paralyzed, on my head. I felt it like a baptism. He kept rubbing my head and my scarf came loose and fell onto my shoulders and then on the floor. I laid my cheek in his lap and he gripped the hair at the nape of my neck between his fingers and I heard him ask me, the words all muddy-sounding and sorrowing, sounding the way tears would if tears could talk, in a voice like that, that sounded better to me than anything I'd heard in as long as I can remember, he asked me, "Don't leave me, Aisha, never leave me. Please stay."

Tameka

FOR my sixteenth birthday, I asked for and got a full-length mahogany-framed mirror. In it now I see my body, speckled with water from the shower. I've got mama's small breasts and as I hold them, they barely fill up my palms. My waist is tiny and broadens into hips set high and, I like to think, proud, as I look at myself sideways. Sometimes I'm sure this body doesn't belong to me. And each time I look at it this close, it's different. I've got my grandmother's face, set and real determined.

They're beginning to use the word "woman" sometimes when they talk about me. "You're a young woman now, not a girl anymore." "Soon you'll be a woman," my grandmother, who lives with us, tells me as we string beans or wash greens at the kitchen table. I hear the words and I wonder what they mean. But no one will tell me. My father won't or can't, I don't know which. Now he can talk almost as good as before. But there's something missing, some feeling we all listen for every time he talks. Maybe because of what he lost, he can't tell me what I need to know and what I can't just yet anyway, ask. I watch my parents, mama who sometimes lets her hand play gently at the back of daddy's neck. And daddy, who looks at mama sometimes like she's somebody he just met but knows already that he wants. I watch them and understand what I see.

Mama helps run the stores and is studying at City College part-time. I pick up the towel bunched at my feet and wrap it around my body as I sit on the edge of the bed and I think about Aunt Crystal and Aunt Serena. Maybe they can tell me what the words mean. My eyes look for the picture Aunt Serena cut out of the newspaper and sent us, now stuck on my bulletin board. It shows her being made chief of a village by a group of women. And next to it is the picture she sent us of the baby she had a year ago, the Alhaji's child. Aunt Serena invited us all to come to visit her, but it's just me who's going. Mama says she wants to go to summer school and daddy won't go all that way without her. So they'll send me in their place. And when I get there I'll ask Aunt Serena what mama and my grandmother mean, what it's like to be a woman and how it feels. Aunt Crystal dedicated her last book to me. Mama is teaching me how to weave on the loom. And as I zip up my skirt, my body shivers and I feel what I think is the answer. I'll tell each of them and listen to what they say. Maybe then they'll tell me what the answer is. At least now, I know where it's found.